The Asylum Gates
By Candace Shattuck

Dedication

This book is dedicated to my friend, Morgan (Momo) Brown. She has always been a great inspiration and has helped me through many times of uncertainty with my writing. This book was created as a tribute to the website she made: theasylumgates.webs.com, and while the site no longer is active, I hope that through this book, it can live on.

Disclaimer

This is a work of fiction. Names, characters, business, events, and incidents are the products of the author's imagination. Any resemblance to actual persons, living or dead, or actual events is purely coincidental.

Warning:

Contains violence and some graphic descriptions. May be triggering for some readers.

To Whoever Finds This,

Hello, I suppose I should introduce myself. My name is Magyk. I was never particularly good at writing letters. I am more of a storyteller. I needed to document our journey before it was too late. I have found myself in a sort of hell...and I will admit this is quite the predicament. However, I know I won't be here much longer and since I have seen how our journey ends, I need to document it so our story can be told and not just the story they will want you to believe. So, in doing that...I wasn't sure where to start. So, I thought I would start with one of my closest friends and longest companions, Eira. Now the story I am about to tell you is long before we met, but I feel it is important to fully understand her and her part in all this. But before we begin, I feel it is important to note that I am not the Magyk spoken of in the story I am about to tell. This is the story of my eternal friend, Eira. Unfortunately, I never had the fortune of meeting Eira's sister, but I am sure I would have liked her. I am getting sidetracked, though. We should get to the story while there is still time left. Please read ahead. Make sure our story is known. Make sure our voice is heard.

Love Always Wins,

Magyk Storm Candles

Contents

Chapter 1: The Escape

She had no idea how long she had been running or how much farther she would have to go as she stood in the alleyway dripping with blood. Was she cut? No. That would be impossible, but she checked herself anyway. She stared out into the darkness at the people around her. They were laying there. Lifeless. They stared up at her with their cold, dead eyes…just the way she liked it. She smiled down at them as the shadows moved to collect her weapons and theirs. Of course, she would leave the guns. They were a relatively new creation she saw no use for. Guns were just too simple—too easy to kill with. She preferred the slow, painful death. They were all sent to kill her since she had escaped the testing facility. She knew others had as well. All had been caught. All except her and a patient only known to her as Patient 42. However, that was all she knew about him. She had met none of the other test subjects.

She didn't know where she was now, but a quick survey of her surroundings told her she was in some village. Looking out from the alley, she could see men in doublets and breeches similar to the ones the humans in the facility wore. There was a young girl wearing a long shirt that went to her ankles. *Strange clothing choice,* she thought. She looked down at her own tattered shirt and pants. She looked out of place and was unsure why she didn't seem to fit in.

She was only eight, but she knew how to kill. She knew she differed from the people in this village. Did they even know about the facility? Or the creatures they created and trained? She was born with abilities they couldn't even dream of. She looked innocent and frail, which made people hesitant to attack her, and by the time they realized their mistake…it was too late for them. Few people would look into her eyes. She didn't know for herself, but she had been told they were hypnotizing and could turn into dark flowers. Her captors at the facility had told her it seemed to be a trait in her family. She wondered if they still had other family members there but knew she couldn't sacrifice her freedom to go back for them if they did.

It was a powerful ability to just look someone in the eyes and have them end it all themselves, but that was just one of her abilities. She also had the advantage in fights due to how quickly and silently she could move. Her ability to talk to animals had aided in her escape as she used this ability to cause distractions or find good hiding places. Another useful talent in her escape was her ability to sense or see things before they would happen, as she could predict what would happen and prepare for it. But the most useful of all her abilities had always been having the shadows at her command to fight alongside her or to bring her an arsenal of weapons. With this ability it seemed as though no one could stop her.

She stayed there in the alleyway by what she presumed to be a church. She was covered in the blood of the people who had pursued her. She knew she shouldn't stay long, and the longer she did, the more she risked being caught, but she couldn't help it. She felt she needed to wait, although she did not know what she was waiting for. Maybe she was waiting for someone else to take her back or maybe she was waiting for someone to kill her…maybe she was even hoping they would. Perhaps she was hoping the other escapee would find her or maybe it was just nice not to have to run for a minute. She waited in silence, staring out at the people. No one was coming for her. She was on her own and at least for the moment, she was safe. After all, they would have to be stupid to come to fight her in the shadows where she would be at her strongest.

She shook her head and turned her head up to the full moon above her and laughed. She then turned her attention back to the people lying in the alley. She sighed and knelt. "I am sorry."

She whispered something under her breath, and as she did, the blood from the recent victims drained from them and flowed into the vials she wore around her waist. Then the shadows came up around the people and collected them. She needed their blood. It wasn't a survival thing. She didn't need it to live, but she needed it. As she took one of the vials and drank it, she knew they were watching her. Her beloved friends...her guardian and her tormentor. How he would be proud. How disappointed would he be when he found out that the good inside was dead? The thought made her smile causing blood to trail down her chin.

She didn't know how long she had remained hidden in the alley when she saw him...a masked and robed figure. She had seen him before. There was no mistaking it. He was Patient 42. She knew little about him or his origins, but what she knew scared her. She had rarely seen him in the facility, but when they would go past his room, there was an unsettling sense of darkness and evil coming from the door. Why was he there? Had he escaped like her and the others? Or was he there to hunt her down?

A chill went down her spine when he looked in her direction. He didn't seem to pay any attention to her, but she knew he had seen her and was watching. She waited in the darkness till he was on the church's steps. He seemed preoccupied with something there. She took this chance to slip away. She ran past him and saw he had lifted his mask slightly in the dark. As she moved past him, he glanced in her direction. For a moment, it was as if time had stopped as she glimpsed his face. He was familiar. She knew him. No. That was impossible. It must have been a trick...or was it? She shook her head and laughed silently about how foolish she was being and continued to run. Where she was going, she had no idea. What she knew was she couldn't stop. If she did, she would be dead.

She didn't know how far she had run nor where she had run, but her pursuers were close behind. She didn't know what business Patient 42 had at the church, but the townspeople had learned of their presence because of it. They seemed to think she had something to do with it and had joined the pursuit. She had only stopped to catch her breath, but as she stared at the woods around her, she knew she was lost, and there was nowhere left to run. She would have to stand her ground and fight or she would have to surrender to whatever fate the townspeople had for her. She was preparing herself for the fight, knowing it would inevitably lead to her capture when she saw it. The giant iron gates in the distance. Behind them appeared to be a grand structure. She could make out its silhouette in the darkness. She didn't know how but she knew she would be safe there. She had to get inside those gates somehow. She heard her pursuers approaching. It wasn't that far. Probably just another 4 miles ahead of her. She could make it.

She ran until she thought she couldn't anymore. Looking up at the huge iron gate, she knew she couldn't climb it. She could use her shadows, but that would be too risky. If the townspeople saw her do it and caught her, they may have a worse fate for her than simply returning her to the facility. She approached the gate cautiously, studying the bars and what was inside. She could probably fit between the bars, but she wanted to know what awaited her on the other side.

She gripped the bars and felt the rust against her hands. It seemed as though no one had been near this gate in years or whatever was inside it. Was it abandoned? She stared at the spikes on top of the bars. *Was there bloodshed here?* Something about this place didn't feel natural…like it was a part of another world. There was an old path leading to the building. It was odd looking and out of place. It looked like some weird mixture of brick and stone…but why was it black? She tried to see where it led, but it was so far ahead she almost couldn't see where it led.

The grass was so green in comparison it looked unnatural. She could smell the dew and feel the water in the air. She could see a few dead patches of grass and felt the agony of the Earth they were on screaming inside her head. When she looked up again, she saw that inside the gate, there appeared to be as many trees as in the surrounding forest, but they were all weeping willows. She smiled. She didn't know where she was breaking into, but she knew she would like it there.

She had easily squeezed through the bars and had begun down the path. After walking through the beautiful forest for an hour, she saw a huge building made of faded bricks and tons of windows. It was huge. She smiled happily. Was this the building she had seen in the forest? It looked old and abandoned, and yet she could feel life coming from inside of it. The windows made her so happy. Oh, how she loved windows. There were no windows in the facility; if she was caught, she might never see the light again. The only sound she could hear was the sound of the crickets chirping and the fading voices of her pursuers. She knew they were too far away to see her now and would never find her. How she longed to go inside the building, to be safe there, but she knew she could not. Whoever was inside would never accept her, but she couldn't stay out here forever either.

The stairs leading to the massive door were old and broken, but what intrigued her the most was the giant tower with the clock that led straight up above the door. She could smell the people inside. She could sense both great evil and good emanating from it. She stared at the office window above the huge wooden double doors. The light came on and she hid herself quickly when she saw movement in the window.

She stared up at the window with her young eyes glistening. There was a person in the window staring down at her. *Can she see me? No…that would be impossible. I am cloaked. No human should be able to see me.* But then why did she feel as if this person was staring right through her? She stared back. It appeared to be a young girl, maybe early twenties. She appeared to be of average height. She stood there watching in what appeared to be a black and white sweater and a cloak. She was beautiful. Her hair was black and appeared to be spiked. She couldn't see her eyes as her bangs covered them, but the darkness of her hair greatly contrasted her skin's paleness and ruby red lips. She could sense she was trying to be professional, but the feeling she gave off was of an inner tortured, fun-loving soul.

Suddenly the girl turned and disappeared out of sight. The big wooden doors opened and she came outside. She walked gracefully in Eira's direction. Seeing her up close made Eira believe she was the most beautiful creature she had ever seen. She had seen little beauty in this world. She approached the spot where Eira was hiding. She stared into the shadows. *Can she see me?* She seemed to look right at Eira. Eira stared back, and after a while, Eira gave a sigh of submission and revealed herself. There was no use hiding from this one. She was different.

The girl leaned forward and crouched down to meet Eira's eyes. Eira hesitantly looked up into her eyes, scared of what she would find. As she did, she noticed that her eyes were the most beautiful shade she had ever seen, and she knew there was no color she could use to describe them adequately. At that moment, she felt safe, loved, and wanted. These were feelings Eira had never known before. Feelings she both feared and yet, a part of her never wanted them to go away.

This girl stared back into Eira's eyes. They were not the eyes of a child. They were filled with a deep sorrow and a longing that nothing could ever wash away. She could see a pain so deep she was not sure if even the mighty powers of the universe could fix it. These were the eyes of a tortured soul, a cold-blooded killer, and yet behind it all, she could see a glimpse of joy, hope, and longing that only this girl could understand and Eira somehow knew she did.

There was a long silence between the two before the girl finally spoke. "And who might you be, sweetheart?"

Eira hesitated at first, breaking eye contact before finally stuttering, "M-my name is E-Eira…Eira Candles." She bit her lip, silently praying the girl would not recognize her name. "May I ask what your name is?"

"My name? Why, I am Miss Cameron, dear. Please don't be afraid. Do you have any idea where you are, Eira?"

She knew by the tone in her voice she had recognized her name, but she didn't seem afraid of her and she didn't seem to be condemning. Eira was curious about this but simply shook her head.

"You are at Bathory Asylum, my dear. I am the headmistress here. You must be a long way from home. May I ask where you came from?"

Miss Cameron was smiling. Strangely it warmed Eira and made her forget her fear of trusting new people. "I came from a testing facility. I escaped. A lot of us did. Although only me and one other managed to escape untouched."

Suddenly Eira's eyes seemed to grow big. Miss Cameron's face went from a look of amusement to one of concern. "What is wrong, my dear?"

Eira wiped at her eyes. What was this? Tears? She had never had tears before. "You…you aren't going to send me back there are you?"

Miss Cameron gave a light-hearted chuckle. "Why of course not, deary. Actually, I was thinking you could stay here. With me. With us. With our whole screwed-up family. After all, everyone is welcome here at Bathory. You would like that, yes?"

Eira nodded. Miss Cameron reached out her hand. Eira looked at it and back at Miss Cameron before hesitantly reaching out and taking Miss Cameron's hand. She slowly followed her inside, as it began to rain.

Chapter 2: Welcome to Bathory

Beyond the door, there was a beautiful spiral staircase. It appeared to be made of iron. The moonlight reflected down from the window above it made it appear as though the staircase had wings. Behind the staircase was another set of massive doors, but she didn't know what they were for. To either side of them was what appeared to be hallway after hallway filled with doors. This place was so much bigger than the facility. It had to be or maybe she had never been allowed to see much of the facility. She felt like she could explore forever and never explore the same place twice. As they approached the staircase, the doors opened and she saw what appeared to be a grand ballroom or feasting hall. A huge chandelier hung from the ceiling, and on the far wall, there was a fireplace and above it was a picture of a middle-aged man who reminded her of Miss Cameron, but before she could ask or see who had opened the door, Miss Cameron whisked her away.

They went up the stairs into the office. As they entered the office, she noticed the only light source seemed to be a small lamp device that reminded Eira of torches. Eira had seen nothing like it. It was a strange light source compared to the candlelit village she had gone through. The room smelled of cherry wood, and in that moment, Eira felt at home.

Eira stood in awe. Everything in this room was made of cherry wood. Everything but the walls, that is. There was a beautiful desk in the center of the room with a comfortable-looking chair in front of it. There were two chairs on the opposite side. They were all angled so the people sitting in them could easily make eye contact while they worked or conversed. Off to the right, she could see a beautiful fireplace. Oh, how she wished to see it lit up. To watch the fire burn To listen to it crack as it danced before her eyes. Off to the left, there were very dark-looking shelves. They appeared to be coated in something, but Eira didn't know what. It was put there to hide the scent of blood, but blood was one thing you couldn't hide from Eira. She knew it better than she knew anything else. After all, blood was her life.

She shook her head, trying to hold on to her sanity as the horrid screaming began. The voices were back. She was fighting the urge to claw at her ears. Miss Cameron sat down behind the desk and motioned Eira to sit. As Eira was taking her seat, she noticed the door to the left of the shelves. She tilted her head slightly, wondering what the door led to. Something told her it was not like the other doors.

Eira sat in silence, watching the door…waiting. What she was waiting for, she had no idea. Finally, Miss Cameron broke the silence, forcing her to focus on her. "So, what brings you to Bathory Asylum, young Eira? Do you need anything to eat or drink?"

Miss Cameron opened a drawer in her desk and pulled out her laptop. This technology was something Eira had seen in the facility, but it seemed out of place now that she had been out in the real world. The town she had come across looked too primitive to have such things. Curious.

Miss Cameron opened the laptop and busied herself, but with what Eira had no clue, so she kept staring at her with a curious expression. Miss Cameron kept glancing at her in such a way that Eira got a sinking feeling she was working on something dealing with her. Miss Cameron reached back into the drawer and pulled out a file. She laid it on the desk. The file had Eira's name on it. *How does she have a file about me? Does she work with the facility? Is she one of them?*

Finally, Eira answered her question, "No…I do not need anything. I am…fine…"

Miss Cameron looked up at her and Eira knew she didn't believe her. Eira looked like she hadn't eaten in weeks. Miss Cameron knew better than to call a patient a liar out right so she just nodded her head.

"And as for why I am here…I told you already…I escaped the testing facility. I had to get away. Surely you can understand that?"

Miss Cameron nodded. "All right then. I just have a few questions for you. If you are willing to answer them?"

"Of course, madam," Eira responded.

"All right, then tell me, dear, were you harmed?"

"I guess that is one way of looking at it."

"That is not what I asked you."

"I do not know how to answer."

"Well, my child, do you feel you were harmed in any way?"

"It is complicated. They were good to me but…"

"But?"

Eira remained silent.

"Dear, it is okay. You can tell me what is wrong." Miss Cameron reached for her hand, but Eira moved further away.

Miss Cameron sat back in her chair. From what she knew about Eira, she would never admit she had been hurt or was hurting. She would never let herself be that vulnerable. However, she knew harm had been done to the child. Miss Cameron knew about the facility she came from enough to know that and if she had not been harmed, she would not have wanted to escape. Miss Cameron typed something into her computer.

After a little while, Miss Cameron asked, "So, Eira, tell me do you know who kept you in the facility? Or why you were there?"

Eira sat in silence for a while as if contemplating. Finally, she responded, "I do not know who kept me. They seemed to be important. I do not know enough about humans to make an adequate conclusion as to their importance, though. As for why, ma'am, I could not tell you. However, I think it has something to do with my father…whoever he is."

Miss Cameron looked at her with curiosity. "May I inquire as to why you think it had something to do with your father?" "I overheard the man in charge of me say that out of the children they had, I was the most promising. He said they could not duplicate the process adequately if my father did not return. But he seemed sure he would come back."

"Was he the one who helped you escape?"

"No. I do not know who let me out."

Eira looked at Miss Cameron suspiciously. *Why is she asking me these questions?* Miss Cameron typed more on her computer before asking, "Tell me, dear, what did they do to you?"

Eira tensed. Miss Cameron stared at her and then she heard it. Footsteps and they were coming closer to her office door. Miss Cameron quickly closed the computer and put it and the file back into the drawer. "Eira, go into that room and don't come out till I tell you to."

Eira quickly hurried to obey Miss Cameron.

The room she had entered was black and white. Eira froze for a minute, taking in the sudden change of color. This room also appeared to be furnished with cherry wood painted to match the color scheme. On the left back corner, she could see a bed under the window with a small dresser on the right. At the end of the bed, a chest reminded Eira of the toy chests she had heard so much about. On the right was a small closet, and at the back of the room was another small window except this one didn't seem to peer outside. *I wonder what the purpose of that window is.* She stepped toward it, then decided not to. *That can wait. I need to know what is going on out there.*

She turned around and noticed that the pure white carpet had a familiar stain on it. There was blood on the floor. Just then, she picked up another familiar smell…but could it be? She followed the smell with her eyes, and that is when she noticed under the dresser there was a small black cat with gleaming yellow eyes. The cat wore a small red collar with a golden tag reading Ember. She stared at the cat. She wanted to talk to it and make friends with it. She approached the cat, but then she heard the office door open. It sounded as if someone walked in and then the door slammed shut. She quickly made her way back to the door.

She pressed her ear against the door. She could smell rainwater. Just then, she heard the roaring storm outside for the first time since she had entered the asylum or perhaps, she had been too preoccupied to pay it much mind. There was something off about the smell. The rainwater smell was fused with the smell of blood…both old and new. Eira suspected that whoever had entered the office had some encounter…one in which the other party was no longer a part of this world. *Could it be the other escapee?* She grabbed the doorknob and turned it but remembered Miss Cameron's orders and released it reluctantly.

She knew they were talking, but she couldn't hear them. *Could it be the storm? No. I have never experienced this problem due to a storm before, so why would I now? Maybe there is just something off about this room.* She heard the scraping of a chair as it was being pulled out. Perhaps the man was sitting down. The next thing she heard was something dangling in the wind. It sounded like a necklace. The storm raged louder. Then suddenly she heard a familiar voice…a man's voice. He was calling her name. Had he followed her here? His voice was so familiar, but she couldn't think of who it was at this moment.

Eira listened intently. She heard the door open and close. She heard the drawer open and some paper rustling about. Just then, she noticed the smell of fire burning and could hear it crackling with the storm. Before she knew it, Miss Cameron opened the door and Eira stumbled out of the room. Miss Cameron helped her up and pushed her quickly out of the office and into the hallway. Bloodied footprints led from the office down the stairs.

Miss Cameron led her quickly down the stairs and down the hall on the right. She opened a door with a blue handle and led her silently inside. "This is where you will be staying, Eira. If you need anything, you know where to find me."

"I thought you wanted to know what they did to me?"

"I do, sweety, but some other time, okay? I have things I must take care of. Maybe we can finish tomorrow?"

Eira nodded silently.

"Good night, Eira."

"Good night," Eira replied. Once Miss Cameron closed the door, she added, "And dreadful nightmares to you."

Miss Cameron froze outside the door. She knew that phrase, but where had this girl heard it?

She sighed and looked around the big empty room. *I wonder if this room is as big as it appears to be or if it is an illusion made by the white walls.* All this white made her shiver. The only comfort this room seemed to have for her was the cherry wood floor and the parts of the walls that were fading. She ran over to the far-left corner and looked at the bed. The sheets were dark and starry looking, and the pillows were soft to the touch. She sat down on the bed and smiled. The expression confused her. She touched her lips slowly. What was this strange sensation? She didn't smile often. When she had, it had only been due to bloodshed. What was this strange feeling she was experiencing? She didn't know what she was feeling, and she wasn't sure if she liked it, but she somehow knew it was a good feeling. She had never had a bed before and would have gladly slept on the floor if it meant never having to go back where she came from.

She sat there smoothing the sheets, wiping the dust from them. She reached for the dresser by the bed and wiped it free of dust. This room was old and didn't appear to have been used in a long time. And yet, as she touched it, she felt the warmth of the life that had once been there. Just then, she saw a young girl with black spiked hair giggling and laughing in the room as if she were playing some game. She removed her hand from the dresser and the image faded. She looked at the small closet that still had some clothing hanging up. Underneath, some boxes appeared to have more clothing in it. She thought about investigating but then decided against it. It wasn't polite to go through the things of others without their permission.

Instead, she slowly laid down on her back and stared at the ceiling. There was a dusty fan-like object hanging from the ceiling. It was already off, and she had no intention of ever turning on the light or fan ever again. She just lied there and for the first time, she noticed the walls had designs on them, but the designs had faded. *I wonder whose room this was. Had Miss Cameron had someone special to her in this room? Or was the girl she had seen Miss Cameron herself?* Eira shook her head and sighed. She rolled over and looked out the window above the dresser. She curled up into the tightest ball she could and wrapped the blankets around her...and finally closed her eyes...

Chapter 3: A Hint of the Past

She opened her eyes. It was about three in the morning. There was no clock in the room, but she knew the time instinctively. Although she had no idea how. She sighed and sat up in the bed. She backed up as far as she could into the corner and sat there in the dark, silently thinking.

She had done this before, sitting in the corner in a ball or crouching, but always staring...waiting to pounce. She didn't know her parents but what she knew was from her older brother. He used to share a cell with her till they took him away one day and he didn't come back. He had always been there for her, but whether he was her brother or just someone she had attached to, she didn't know. Only he knew.

He had told her many times about their parents. He told her about how beautiful their mother was. He had said she had jet black hair that flowed down her back, contrasting with her snow-white skin. He told her that her eyes were so dark you couldn't tell if she had any pupils but that they were deep. He used to tell her she looked a lot like her, except she was frailer than her mother was. Eira had always been glad there weren't any mirrors in the facility. Eira was always scared to know what she looked like because she feared she would never live up to the beauty he described. She sighed again and stared down at her dirt and blood-stained skin. How could such a wonderful and beautiful creature bring forth such an ugly, vile, evil thing such as herself?

She had always wanted to meet her mother, but when she had expressed this desire to him, he had gotten angry with her. She was only three at the time and didn't understand, but when she got a little older, he explained that it would be impossible for her to see their mother. She had inquired as to why. He told her that their mother was sick from everything they had done to her in the facility, and as a result, she and the other child had to be transferred to the other facility. He never specified what they had done, but she had seen enough of what went on in this facility to know they had made her sick. She knew little about the other facility, but she had always hoped it was better than the one they were in.

She did not know that her mother was the beginning of their project. They had established these two facilities. They had created a child. A boy. He was a perfect specimen and had been admitted to Project Damen. Seeing as how it worked so well the first time, they tried again. However, this time the experiment didn't go so well, and she was going to die. Her father had not been ok with this as they had fallen in love. So, he tried to end the pregnancy by cutting out the experimental children from her when she was only five and a half months pregnant. The man who had taken her had told him to leave her there. No one would know. They would think the experiment had gone wrong, and no one would be there to hear her scream. He had refused. The man had taken her as she appeared to be strong, figuring the woman and other child would die. That was the night her father disappeared, abandoning her and her brother and took her mother and the other child north where he had built a second facility secretly.

Whether it was intended or not, he had fallen in love with the woman who was her mother. He couldn't bear to watch her die, so he knew he had to save her. The others at this facility had already decided that she and the other child would die, and if they survived, they would be in danger. So, he had taken them away. He had wanted to take his other two children with him as well, but unfortunately, they had taken the other baby and the child would be too far away. If he went to get them now, the woman and the child she clung to in her arms would die before he got back. So, he needed to get them out of there. He could always return later for the other two. They were strong. They would survive.

Everyone had assumed that the other two were dead, but none knew for sure. However, they knew that eventually he would return for his other two children. Meanwhile, they kept trying to recreate their experiment. That is how Eira had ended up in the care of the facility. She didn't know anyone's name there but the man who cared for her seemed to think she was special.

She had spent so many nights afraid to sleep. Waiting for him to return and wondering if he would. She was afraid if she closed her eyes, they would take her again. She had spent so many long hours in that cell she could almost feel the cold stone walls caked in dirt and dried blood. She could almost taste the moldy air. She could see the cold metal door. There was no window to peer outside. How many times had she stared at that door, silently begging for her brother to return and wondering when they would remember she was there and take her away again.

She couldn't count how many times she had woken up with her hands chained above her head and her legs chained beyond movement. She felt the cold metal of the chains digging into her skin. The warm blood slowly flowing from her wrists. She shivered as if she could feel the cold air again. Sometimes she couldn't bear remembering what they had done to her. Other times it was the memory of her screaming and begging them to stop that made her feel ashamed.

The "scientist", as he referred to himself, was a sick man. She couldn't remember much about him, but he seemed to like cold, dark rooms. He had seemed to think she was special or at least she was special to him. He had always called her his child, but she knew he wasn't her father. Every time he spoke, his voice sent shivers down her spine. They knew that their drugs would not affect her. He always began her torture slowly, trailing his fingers

23

slowly up her leg to her inner thigh. He would make a small turn to go around her hip and up her stomach before trailing up to her neck, grabbing her and forcing her head to look up into his eyes. His cold blue eyes...

She shivered. His eyes had always sent shivers through her. They seemed inhuman. They almost didn't seem real. His smile revealed his sharpened teeth. She hated his smile. She hated him. She tried to make that known by her defiance, but he only seemed to admire her more because of the defiance he saw in her eyes. He would always push her head to the side and slice his razor-sharp nails down her back. No matter how hard she tried not to respond, she would always let out a pain-filled growl. Then he would take out his knives...

Just then her hands found something that snapped her back to the present. It was cold and felt like leather. She pulled it forward and heard something rattle...like the sound of rusty chains. She kept pulling until she uncovered the leather restraints and chains attached to the bed. She tried to move the bed to figure out where they were connected, but the bed seemed to be bolted to the floor. The restraints appeared to be covered in dried blood. She dropped the leather restraints back down where she had found them. What had happened here?

She waited for what must have been hours huddled in the corner before she heard the doorknob move. As the door slowly creaked open, she just sat there in the dark. A shadowed figure entered the room slowly. She didn't know if she was awake or if this was a dream or even where she was anymore. She held her breath, afraid it was him again like in all her dreams. Her tormentor. Her master.

She hadn't always been his. He had appeared sometime in the past year when they took her brother. He was like an imaginary friend as no one else saw him, nor did he give her a name. She felt like he wanted to kill her. She could see it in his eyes as she had huddled in her corner. She didn't know who he was or why he had never tried to harm her, but she knew he didn't like her and waited for him to end her existence.

She had looked into his cold eyes and had smiled back. Did he know she was praying he would end her existence? One day she thought for sure he would, but something was different that day. He came in and his eyes were not cold or distant but sad and remorseful. He came close to her and knelt down before her. He had asked her forgiveness and promised to protect her.

She had extended her hand in friendship with this promise and in the moment their hands touched, she felt as if they had become one. Her tortured soul and his. They would guard each other always. Little did she know this would go on for eternity. He had stolen her heart. She was his.

The few months before her escape were as torturous as the rest of her stay. Her new guardian had orders not to intervene from whoever he served and could only provide some comfort afterwards. Perhaps he had freed her? She let out a small, frustrated chuckle. She was free from the facility now, but she was still dealing with the aftermath of it. The voices and hallucinations. The nightmares. The flashbacks and sensations. They wouldn't leave her alone and she had a feeling they weren't going away. Would she ever be free?

She sat in silence and waited for the shadow to reveal itself. It was strange that she could not see who it was. She wondered if they could hide in the shadows as she did. The figure approached the dresser and then a candle was lit on the dresser and then the figure turned around. The light flickered, revealing Miss Cameron's smiling face. She stared down at Eira. "Good Morning, Eira. I trust you slept well. It is seven o'clock and time to wake up, darling." She paused briefly. "It looks like you have been up for a while. How long have you been sitting there?"

"Since roughly three o'clock..." she responded, curling tighter.

Miss Cameron waited for a moment trying to decide if she should address the problem or just leave it for now. She sighed. "Well, hurry up and get dressed. Breakfast is waiting for you. I will take you down to the cafeteria."

Eira didn't move

"Well, go on...there are clothes in the closet."

Eira slowly moved, feeling warmer from Miss Cameron's energy. Did she know about what had happened to her? No. How could she? No one believed her even when she woke with marks to prove it. They said she had done it to herself for attention.

She crossed over to the closet slowly looking at the stuff hanging on the rack. She tilted her head slowly. The clothes were her size, but when she had gone to bed, they had looked too big. Had Miss Cameron come into the room and switched them out? No. She would have woken up.

She glanced in Miss Cameron's direction, but Miss Cameron just stood there, smiling. She turned back towards the clothes and reached up and pulled down a pair of black pants. She slipped them on and then removed her blood-stained dress, replacing it with a dark shirt. She walked over to the dresser and put on her fingerless gloves and her boots. Miss Cameron reached out her hand and Eira took her cloak from her and wrapped it around herself before following her out of the room.

Miss Cameron watched her, remembering herself as a child. She couldn't help but notice how similar this girl was to that little girl she once knew. And yet she had become so different. What had they done to her? Only Miss Cameron and Eira knew the answer to that. Miss Cameron's visitor had dropped off the records of her stay in the facility, both written and video recordings. He had hoped it would aid in the finding of the child, which Miss Cameron had no intention of aiding in. However, she could not let Eira know what had transpired. The child had been traumatized enough and Miss Cameron did not want the girl to mistrust her.

She had watched the girl as she picked out clothes and noticed the girl was wrapped in bandages. For a moment, her smile faded. They were about to leave the room when Miss Cameron went over to the bed. "Come here, dear. I will brush your hair."

Eira quietly walked over to the bed and sat down. Miss Cameron sat beside her and gently brushed her hair. Eira pulled her cloak tighter around herself, trying to hide. She couldn't help but wonder if Miss Cameron had noticed. Everything was silent. Then Miss Cameron spoke. "What are those bandages for, dear?"

Eira tensed, tightening her grip on the cloak. "W-what bandages?"

"The ones you have covering your skin. The ones you are hiding right now, beneath the cloak."

Eira froze. She had noticed. "The cloak is not to hide the bandages."

"Then what is it for, dear?"

"The same thing the bandages are for. To hide my skin…so I don't have to remember what he did to me…"

"And what did he do to you?"

Eira contemplated how to answer that question. The answer was simple, but she could not make herself voice it. The words are there, but she found herself mute. She knew she would have to tell Miss Cameron something eventually but for right now she could only give her a general idea. "Bad things, Miss Cameron. Bad things. Things that no one should have to face...human or otherwise..."

Miss Cameron was silent. Did the girl understand she was not human?

Finally, Eira broke the silence. "These newer bandages are from the bad man..."

"What bad man? The one who hurt you?"

"No. The one in my dreams. He turns your reality into his."

Everything was silent. The only sound was the brush slowly gliding through Eira's long black hair. After a while, Eira spoke. "Miss Cameron?"

"Yes, sweetheart?"

"May I ask you a question?"

"Why, of course, dear. You just did."

Eira giggled a little. "What are the restraints for?"

Miss Cameron stopped moving. She hesitated for a moment, then continued to brush her hair. "Restraints?"

"The ones attached to the bed?"

Miss Cameron sat still. Her face grew dim as her smile faded. Eira turned and stared up at Miss Cameron's empty eyes. She recognized that look. She was remembering something. Eira didn't know what it was, but she knew it was unpleasant.

Suddenly Miss Cameron's face shot up and she took Eira's hand and ushered her out the door, half dragging her down the hallway to where the stairwell was. Once they reached the bottom of the stairs, they turned toward the large double doors. Miss Cameron pushed them open and deposited Eira inside. There was a table inside with eleven people around it. Eira tilted her head and asked, "Where is everybody?"

Miss Cameron smiled. "Don't worry about that."

Miss Cameron turned to leave. Eira grabbed her shirt tightly. "You aren't leaving me, are you?"

"I must go to the watch tower now. The inmates need me. You will be just fine, dear." With that, she was gone, leaving Eira alone.

Chapter 4: Mastema

She stood there in silence, unsure of what to do. She felt a small hand tap her shoulder. She turned around and there was a girl about her height standing behind her. How had she gotten there? She had long black hair that covered her eyes and a torn, faded black gown on. Her skin looked almost as pale if not paler than Eira's. The girl spoke. "Hello, Eira. My name is Mastema."

"Hello? How do you know…"

Mastema cut her off. "Your name? I know a lot of things, Eira."

Eira nodded her head slowly. The girl appeared to have a silhouette of wings behind her. Mastema smiled as if she knew what Eira was thinking. "So you see it?"

"See what?"

"My wings."

Eira did not respond. Mastema smiled again. "Don't worry, you will get yours eventually. It comes as the power inside matures. Although when it does happen, I do suggest you keep them cloaked. Others tend to freak out a bit."

Eira did not know how to respond, so she changed the subject. "So, who are all these people?"

"These are the patients of Bathory Asylum or at least the ones who have joined us. The others won't come down."

"Why not?"

"They have their reasons. Shall I tell you who everyone is?"

Eira nodded.

"The girls over there are Midnight and Eden's Promise. They usually hang out together and stick to themselves. Maybe they have something to hide, but that is speculation. What we do know is that Midnight came from the other facility and Eden's Promise showed up with her, but we do not know for sure where she came from."

Eira looked where she was pointing. The girl she had called Midnight was consumed in some drawing or writing she was doing while she was eating. She had bright red hair, and her skin was pale, almost abnormally so. Her eyes were darker than the night sky, which matched the lipstick she was wearing. She had a long purple dress on and bandages on her arm. She was a young girl. Probably in her late teens, maybe early twenties. She was exceptionally beautiful.

Sitting next to her was a girl with a similar skin tone and lipstick color, but she had long blond hair. Eira also noted she was wearing mostly black and didn't seem interested in eating. She was watching Midnight work and was swirling the food around but never actually ate. Suddenly Midnight looked up and saw Eira watching, and they both took off.

Eira turned to look at Mastema, who seemed to sense her confusion. Mastema sighed. "Like I said, they like to be left alone. Midnight seems a little sensitive to others' presence and doesn't like anyone being nosy." Eira objected. She wasn't trying to be nosy, but Mastema cut her off before she could say anything. "Even if they don't mean it that way. Anyways, the other girl at the table is Kas. She came from the same facility as the Midnight. The main thing we know about her is that she likes ancient Egypt."

Kas was sitting there quietly with her head down. She was pale like the other two, with long black hair covering her eyes. Eira couldn't help but notice she looked so frail. She wore a white dress, and her limbs looked so small under it. She wondered what had happened to her. Suddenly Kas looked up. Eira was worried this girl would respond negatively to her, too, so she quickly averted her gaze. When she did, she noticed a girl standing by the window. "Who is that?"

"Her name is Mas. Not much is known about her. She always wears this cloak. She seems determined to figure something out, but I am not really sure what it is she hopes to uncover. She is very much like her sister Maddy Hellfire. They look identical, but Maddy has a darker complexion than Mas. Also, Maddy has blue eyes while Mas has darker eyes. It is strange since they are supposed to be identical twins. Do not worry. You will meet Maddy, Phoenix, Lily, and Marie later."

Eira sat down with Mastema. Neither of them gathered food to eat. Why Mastema didn't Eira didn't know, but for Eira, it was simply because the human food being served didn't appeal to her today. Eira looked at Mastema. "So, is everyone here from the other facility?"

Mastema shook her head. "You, me and Phoenix all seem to be from the same place. Also, like I said, no one knows where Eden's Promise came from."

"I thought the other facility was a good place. Why are there so many people here from there? I always heard that the other facility was like a utopia. If that is true, why would so many people want to leave?"

Mastema didn't answer.

After everyone had eaten, Mastema dismissed herself. Eira busied herself collecting the dishes. She took them to the kitchen and offered to help, but they dismissed her. So, she decided it was better for her to return to her room.

After a while, she went to Miss Cameron's office. When she arrived, she raised her hand to knock, but before she could, she heard movement on the other side, indicating Miss Cameron knew she was there. Suddenly she heard Miss Cameron's voice telling her to come in. Eira slowly pushed open the door and stepped inside. She turned to close the door. She tried to make it as silent as possible.

Miss Cameron motioned to a chair. "Take a seat, dear."

Eira nodded and obediently did as she was instructed. She wanted to talk but couldn't bring herself to, so she stared at her hands. Miss Cameron waited to see if Eira would speak. When she did not, she decided she would have to say something if the young girl was going to talk. "What is on your mind, young one?"

Eira remained silent, but Miss Cameron noticed her neck twitched a bit, and she had a strange look on her face. It appeared as though the young girl was arguing within herself. Miss Cameron could sense there was still a hint of the small good-hearted child but that it was at odds with the murderous demon she had become.

Suddenly Eira whispered silently, "I got away…"

She went quiet again. Miss Cameron could tell the child had some internal conflict. She had been through quite a lot. Miss Cameron knew from the others she had taken in from both facilities that it wasn't pleasant in the facilities. Although, the one Eira came from was notably worse and the other facility was less bad. The ones she took in from the project Eira had been in had suffered extreme mental and physical abuse and, in some cases, had even been subjected to sexual abuse. Perhaps that is what the girl was struggling with. To help her like she had promised her mother, she would need to know. But that would take time and patience.

Chapter 5: Intake

The next day at mealtime Eira noticed that Eden's Promise was by herself, so she went over to her. "Hello, my name is Eira."

"My name is Eden."

"Well, Eden, it is a pleasure to meet you. Would you like to join me and Mastema?"

She stared at the ground, sheepishly. "Sure…"

Eden sat beside her silently. The silence felt awkward, so Eira tried to be friendly again, even though it was not her strong suit. "So, how long have you been here?"

Neither girl answered. Mastema grunted. This kind of talk was not permitted, but even if she had wanted to answer, she honestly couldn't remember how long she had been here. Eira sighed. "I just got here."

Silence. Eira decided it was probably pointless to pursue a conversation. Neither Mastema nor Eden seemed very social today. After a while, she noticed that Eden was only picking at her food but wasn't eating it. She watched her for a minute before asking, "You don't seem interested in the food?"

"Yeah, I don't eat much. You don't look like you do either."

Eira didn't know what to say. It was true she ate little, but she had never had much to eat either. They all sat and ate in silence. There was a silent tension between Mastema and Eden. Eira couldn't wait for mealtime to be over. After mealtime, Miss Cameron said that she would come collect her to show her around. It would be nice to be around a friendly face for a while. Mastema kept her head down. Eden seemed to glare at her. Eira sat between them, unsure of what to do about the tension. Finally,

Miss Cameron came into the room and motioned for Eira to follow her.

Miss Cameron took her back into her office and they sat down together. They sat in silence for a while as Miss Cameron messed with some files and typed on her computer. Eira shifted in her chair and quickly looked up when Miss Cameron said her name suddenly. "Yes, Miss Cameron?"

"Eira, my dear, we will eventually have to finish our interview. As you know, the people from the facility will not give up until they have you back. If I am going to protect you, I need you to tell me what happened to you. I also need you to answer my questions."

"I know…"

"I know it is sensitive. I know it will be hard, but it is important not only for my records and for me to understand you and your needs but also so you can heal. I want you to know you will always be safe with me. So, we don't have to do this now. I don't know when you will be ready, but when you are, I will be here. However, I cannot hide you from them forever if there is not a substantial cause. It will put the rest of the kids here in danger, and that is something I cannot allow. You do understand?"

"Yes, Miss Cameron."

"If it is anything like some of the other kids who have come here seeking Asylum, then I think I have an idea of how bad things probably were for you. So, if you want, we can just get back to the interview questions."

"No, I think I am ready."

"Are you sure?"

"If I don't do it now…I never will."

"Very well then, Eira. Please go ahead."

Name: Eira Tajna Candles

Date of Birth: Unknown

Identification Number: Patient 3

Facility ID: Project Damen

Intake Questions:

1. Was the patient harmed?

Yes.

Notes: The patient does not like to admit to being harmed. She seems reluctant to talk. Doesn't like vulnerability.

2. Does the patient know who was in charge of the experiment?

No.

Notes: The patient does not seem to know much about the operation or about the outside world.

3. How did the patient escape?

Unknown accomplice let her out. Followed the shadowed figure out of the facility.

4. Who harmed the patient?

Owner of the facility, Scientists, and something the child calls a monster in her dreams.

5. What trauma did the patient endure?

Physical torture, Sexual abuse, Mental games, being forced to kill, Isolation, Emotional trauma, etc.

6. Was anyone else there when the patient suffered the traumatic experience other than the perpetrator?

Unknown. Patient believes another person was there. Someone named Levi. Unclear if he is a real being or a hallucination. Possibly an imaginary friend.

7. Who has the patient told about the situation?

No one.

8. Does the patient have a support system?

No.

9. Was there anyone the patient believes could have helped or protected them but who did nothing?

Patient believes this entity she calls Levi could have helped but did not, even though she regards him as a "friend". She also believes her father could have protected her, but he abandoned her there. She says she does not know if either of her parents are still alive.

10. How long has this gone on?

As long as the patient can remember. Patient is only eight, so probably at least four to six years.

11. Was the trauma reoccurring?

Yes.

12. How did the patient feel before the trauma was inflicted?

Alone and isolated. Raised in the facility, so she probably had no outside experience or ability to be around others.

13. How did the patient feel after the trauma was inflicted?

Patient reports feeling numb, having a low mood, and angry. Shows signs of PTSD. Acts afraid. Seems to carry guilt or shame but refuses to admit to or show it too much. Doesn't like being vulnerable. Hardened spirit and attitude toward the world. Any emotion seems to make her violent.

14. How does the patient feel towards the perpetrators?

She reports feeling angry. Seems to be hurt but won't admit to it. Also admits to feeling attachment to them as she was raised by them.

15. Does the patient feel understood?

No.

16. Description of incident:

Note: The patient has asked not to report this. As it serves no real purpose to do so, we will leave this section as it is until further notice

Chapter 6: Mastema

After they had talked, Eira returned to her room. It had felt good to tell someone what had happened to her. Even though she had not gone into detail and left Miss Cameron with just generalizations she felt good knowing someone else knew and understood what was happening with her. She wondered if she would have felt better had she opened up more and showed Miss Cameron what lies beneath the surface, but that would mean admitting she was weak. She did not want to be perceived as weak. Especially not to Miss Cameron. She hadn't known Miss Cameron for long, but she felt a strange attachment to her and wanted her to like her. Miss Cameron was nice, but would she be if she knew the full truth? That was one answer Eira wasn't sure she wanted.

Eira sat in her room. She felt like a huge weight had been lifted off her shoulders, and yet she had felt this feeling of impending doom since their talk. She couldn't get the memories out of her head either. As they played back in her mind, she could feel their hands and tools on her body. It made her skin crawl, and she absent-mindedly clawed at her arms as if she were trying to get something out. She stared out the window, trying to distract herself, but she still shivered as she heard their voice whispering in her ear. She could almost feel their breath, and she could smell their sweat as if they were in the room with her.

Miss Cameron had suggested that she go spend some time with the other inmates individually to help her find the answers to her questions, as they would know more about what had happened at the facilities than she did. However, Eira was unsure if these other inmates would understand, and even if they did, how would they give her answers about where her parents were? All Eira knew was that she wanted the voices to stop. She wanted to get these memories to go away. And perhaps talking to them was just the distraction she needed to quiet them—at least for a little while.

Miss Cameron sat in her office wondering about the strange new addition to their family. The girl had told her what she had wanted to know, and she did so with such unattachment that it worried Miss Cameron. The girl seemed completely disassociated from any emotion except that of anger. Being raised in the facility would make it hard for her to get her to open up further than that.

Every time she begun to show emotion, she turned away from it. The transition from any other emotion, whether positive or negative, into either numbness or anger was so quick it was hard to tell if the other emotion had ever been there. Miss Cameron knew she would have to get the girl to open up. If she was going to get the girl to do so, she would need her to make friends. One thing that seemed constant among the inmates was that as they became more social and connected with one another the more they opened up, healed and found peace. She hoped the same would be true for Eira.

Miss Cameron had told her to find answers about her parents from the other inmates as she would not understand who or where they are. This was only partly true. Miss Cameron knew who her parents were, but as for where they were, she could only guess. However, she knew that she must make sure the child was safely returned to them. She knew that the other inmates might have the answers she needed, but she also knew that they would not tell her. Yes, all trusted her, but they were too scared of the facilities they came from to tell her all the details, even if she could keep them safe. But Miss Cameron knew they talked amongst each other verbally or telepathically. Miss Cameron could use the girl to find her own answers as the girl hunted for the truth.

Eira felt uncomfortable meeting these other inmates alone, so she thought she would visit Mastema first and see if she would come with her. After searching through the halls, Eira finally came to a black door with Mastema's name written on it. She raised her hand to knock but then the door opened. Eira didn't move. Mastema came to the door and stared at Eira for a second as if waiting for something. When Eira did nothing, Mastema gestured to have her come in. "Please do come in, dear."

Eira walked into the room slowly. *It sure is bright in here.* Mastema smiled and walked over to her vanity. "So we are that kind of creature, are we?"

Eira tilted her head, curious about what she had meant but said nothing. Mastema sat down in the chair in front of the vanity and stared into the mirror. Mirrors were not something Eira was used to and she had always wanted to avoid knowing what she truly looked like. But this mirror was huge and elegant. It made her uncomfortable and yet she was fascinated by it. She looked into the mirror and stared at herself for the first time.

She had long black hair with what appeared to be red highlights and deep dark eyes. Her skin was pale and her lips were rosy. She could see the resemblance between her and her mother from a picture her brother had shown her once. Her clothes weren't torn, bloody, or old anymore. She smiled. For a moment, she thought she could see her mother in the mirror.

Mastema smiled. "Fascinating isn't it?"

41

Eira's attention shifted instantly to Mastema. She could see the girl's face in the mirror. She was only a few years older than Eira, but she was beautiful. "What do you mean?"

"How can mirrors show us the truth about things?"

Eira tilted her head in confusion.

Mastema chuckled. "Mirrors can show us what is hidden, yet they can also show us what we want to see. They can show us truth or lies. They show us how we appear in this world, yet they can also serve as a portal to what lies within our souls. They are so simple and yet so complex, don't you think?"

"I guess so…"

"The balance they have of simplicity and complexity makes them beautiful. Just like you, dear."

Eira couldn't tell if she was insulting or complementing her so she folded her arms and stared at her in silence. Mastema stared at her in the mirror. Eira questioned why Mastema wouldn't actually look at her but decided it was better not to ask. *What does she see anyway?*

She turned her attention to a skull sitting on the table in front of the mirror. It was also facing the mirror. She stared at it. The skull was old and grey and its empty eye sockets were dark, but it looked like something was glowing inside them. Eira shifted to the side to see if she could see the eyes outside of the mirror, but she could not see what made them appear to glow. Mastema noticed that she was staring at her skull. She smiled. "I see you have taken an interest in Methuselah?"

Eira said nothing.

Mastema gestured towards the skull. "Oh, I am sorry. How rude of me! You two haven't been introduced. Eira, this is Methuselah. Methuselah, this is Eira. She is new here."

Everything was silent, but Eira felt a powerful energy coming from the skull she had called Methuselah. She did not know why but she felt as though Methuselah was laughing at her uneasiness. Eira looked away. That was when Eira noticed that she had an odd-looking contraption sitting on the drawer next to some flowers. *I wonder what that is for?* Right above it was a unicorn poster that felt somewhat out of place. Eira chuckled a little bit. She turned to leave, but then suddenly, the strange contraption began to play music. Eira couldn't identify what kind of music it was, but it was dark and yet somehow soothing, so she stopped. When she turned back around, Mastema was behind her and her hair was over her eyes.

Mastema held out a small toy cat that looked like a black cat wearing some Egyptian collar and paint. Eira didn't move. Mastema grabbed her hand and placed the cat in it. Eira tried to hand it back. Mastema shook her head. "No. Methuselah said Bast should come with you now. Methuselah says the answers you seek are on the other side and you will have to cross into the other realm to find what you seek. Bast can help."

"Bast? The other realm? What do you mean?"

"I am sorry I have already said too much." Mastema put her index finger to the center of Eira's forehead. Just remember I will be with you always. If you need me, call. If I have the answer, I will help."

With that, Mastema's door reopened and Eira felt herself removed from the room as if by some unseen force. The door closed behind her, which was curious as Mastema was nowhere near it. Eira looked down at the toy cat. *Well, I guess it is just you and me now.*

Eira returned to her room. The room was dark, just as she liked it. She could see something sitting on the dresser next to the bed. It appeared to be a book. Where did that come from? She walked over to it and picked it up. It read The Holy Bible. Eira sat down on the bed with her legs folded. She held the toy cat on her lap. She didn't know why but she felt a strange connection to it. She had opened the book she had found when she swore, she could hear Mastema's voice; *you shouldn't read in the dark.*

Eira stopped for a minute and considered turning on a light. Being in the dark had never bothered her before. She hesitated, then got up and lit a candle. She placed it on the dresser and repositioned herself down with the book. She read the first line out loud. "In the beginning, God created the heavens and the earth." She paused for a moment as if contemplating something. She continued reading in silence throughout the night.

Chapter 7: Eden's Promise

Eira lost track of time as she read the new book she found. She hadn't moved or come down to eat or left her room since she had found the book. It had been 3 days and Miss Cameron was starting to worry. She knocked on Eira's door. Eira did not answer. Miss Cameron opened the door and walked into the room. She waited to see if Eira would acknowledge her. When she did not, she said her name.

Eira did not look up from the book but said, "I will be with you in a moment."

Everything was quiet until suddenly Eira said, "The mystery of the seven stars which thou sawest in my right hand, and the seven golden candlesticks. The seven stars are the angels of the seven churches: and the seven candlesticks are seven churches."

Eira closed the book and sat it down beside her. Eira turned to look at Miss Cameron. "What is the matter?"

"I was worried, dear. You haven't been out of this room in over three days now."

"Well, you shouldn't worry. I was only reading."

"Do you always read your books in one sitting?"

"Yes. I do not like to get distracted." "And do you always read the last line of the books you read aloud?"

"The first and last, yes. I find it ties things together." "Well, my dear. Since you have finished your book, would you like to join us for breakfast?"

"No. I need time to meditate on what I read. I will come down for dinner, though."

Miss Cameron shook her head. "Ok, dear. Don't stay here another three days or I will drag you out myself, understood?"

"Yes, Miss Cameron."

With that Miss Cameron left the room. Eira remained on her bed. She closed her eyes and took a deep breath.

Eira had gone down to dinner as promised and had spent the time there deciding who she would visit next. She had decided on Eden's Promise. So, she wandered around the corridors looking for her room but could not find one with her name on the door.

Well, this is curious. It is like she doesn't exist. That is when she heard Mastema's voice. "That is because you are looking for the wrong name."

Eira turned around. "Mastema? Where are you?"

In my room.

"Then how can I hear you? And how do you know what I am doing?"

I know lots of things, Eira. I like to communicate through a mental connection the humans call telepathy. I believe you, too, will develop the gift one day. As for watching you, well, you already know how I am doing that.

Eira was confused by that last statement which Mastema seemed to find funny. Eira could hear her chuckling. "Ok, can you tell me what name I am looking for?"

Yes, I can.

Silence.

"Well?"

Well, what?

"You didn't answer the question…"

Oh, but I did, dear. I answered the question you asked. Around here, you need to think and choose your words carefully.

Eira thought for a minute then she asked, "What is Eden's Promise real name?"

She could feel Mastema smiling. *Gabby. Gabby Brokan.*

Eira remembered she had seen a dark fading door with that name on it. She questioned why she called herself Eden's Promise instead of Gabby, but she must have her reasons, and it wasn't Eira's place to question it. She probably wanted to distance herself from her past and who she was as Gabby, and if that was the case, Eira could understand that. She headed off towards the door. She figured Eden would tell her about it in time.

She stood in front of the door for a moment, wondering if it would open like Mastema's did. When it did not, she knocked three times. No one answered. She knocked three more times. Nothing. *Maybe she isn't here.*

She is in there. Knock again.

She knocked three more times. Nothing. Eira was about to give up and stepped away from the door when it opened a crack and she could see Eden's face behind the door.

"Yes?" she said quietly.

"I was wondering if we could talk."

"Talk? With me? About what?" She sounded alarmed.

"Nothing serious, I just wanted to get to know you a little bit. If we are going to be living together, we should at least be able to be courteous to each other, don't you think?"

"I suppose….it's just I don't really like people…."

"Well, if it makes you feel better, I am not really a person."

"You're not?" She looked suspicious.

Eira waited a moment. Then Eden continued. "Ok. I guess it would be ok then."

She opened the door and motioned for Eira to come in. Eira approached the door and froze in front of the doorway. Eden looked at her with an expression she couldn't tell if it was annoyance or confusion. Eira sighed. "I need you to invite me in."

"Oh, ok....um...Eira, would you please come in?"

Eira walked into the room. It was mostly barren except for a bed covered in pink sheets and rows of bookshelves along all the walls. They all seemed covered in different books on angels, demons, and magic. Beside the bed was a stack of binders and one was open on the bed with newspaper clippings that appeared to all be obituaries around it. The floor was littered with empty alcohol containers and cigarette butts. That was odd...wasn't she a little young to have all this stuff? Why did Miss Cameron allow her to have this stuff? Or did she even know?

Eira walked over to the bed. Eden quickly went over and scooped up all the clippings and the binder and shoved it under her bed. Eira tilted her head and walked over to one of the many bookshelves. "You seem to really like paranormal subjects."

Eden looked startled. "W-what do you mean?"

"Your books. They are all about different types of magic and different creatures. On this bookshelf alone, you have books on healing magic, blood magic, vampires, demons, angels, werewolves, mythical creatures, and necromancy, and that's just a small list from this shelf. You also seem to be interested in Obituaries, which is an unusual interest but one I can respect."

"Well, I don't know if it is unusual. I just like to know about the world I am living in."

"The humans would say these things, save the angels and demons, would not have anything to do with the world in which we live. Magic is frowned upon by them and anything dealing with it is deemed evil or simply fantasy."

"Yes, but both of us know they simply do not understand. When it presents itself, they are afraid. The unknown can be scary. Like death."

Eira nodded in silence. She knew what she had said was only partially true. The humans that ran the facility believed in all these things, but from the conversations she had overheard, the people in the village she had gone through would not approve of their activities. She doubted anyone else outside the facilities would either. Eira turned her attention to one obituary on the floor. It looked like it hadn't quite made it under the bed with the others. She stared at it for a minute. She knew that face. It was the face of her mother. And there was a man next to her, maybe her father?

She walked over and crouched down to pick it up. She stared at it. It wasn't an obituary but a newspaper clipping about a missing couple who had been presumed dead. Eden took it quickly and shoved it away.

"What is that?" Eira asked.

"It is nothing. I just felt called to this case."

Eira stared at her, expecting more and finally, she continued. "I just find it interesting when tragedies happen and people go missing, and everyone thinks they are dead, but there is no real way to know. Sometimes they are dead, and sometimes they reappear unscathed from the accident. The mystery of not knowing is what makes it fun. We can make up our own minds as to what the truth is, or we can seek it out. I like to seek the truth."

"Tragedy? Accident? What do you mean?"

Eden said nothing. She just stared at the floor.

"Tell me."

Silence.

Eira grabbed her and shoulders and shook her. "Tell me, now!"

Eden looked at up at her and met her eyes. She looked alarmed. "They were in charge of the second facility. The one that never has runaways. The only ones here from that facility they dropped off here as failed experiments. The facility was destroyed, but they don't know how it was destroyed or who was responsible. A lot of people died in the accident. I am not so sure it was an accident, but the owner of the facility you came from and his wife were there. She was in charge of the other facility. They weren't among the dead. No one knows where they are."

Eira stopped to take in the information. Eden's thoughts seemed jumbled. Why did she always seem so nervous? Was she hiding something? Did this mean that her parents were alive somewhere? Could they have been involved with the facility being destroyed?

Eira turned to go but then stopped. She had one more question that Eden might be able to answer. "When did this "accident" occur?"

"Yesterday…"

Yesterday? That meant that it had happened after the escape. Could one of the other patients be responsible? She needed to find out. She needed to talk to Miss Cameron. She needed time to think.

Eira approached the door, and as she did so Eden's Promise suddenly told her to wait. She turned to see what she wanted, and she held out two binders to her. "You might need this."

Eira looked at the writing on the binders. "Notes on Healing Magic, Blood Magic, Other Realms, Spirit work, Necromancy, Scrying, Telepathy, and Shadow Work."

"This is an odd collection."

"It is all my notes on these subjects from these books. I usually separate the subjects more, but I had a feeling I needed to put this together for someone. I think that someone was you."

Eira took the binder, unsure of what this strange new gift was, but she knew one thing: she had more reading to do. Miss Cameron would not be pleased. But at least it would give her time to compose herself and figure out what she wanted to say when she spoke to Miss Cameron.

When Eira returned to her room, there were more objects setting in there that had not been before. She sat the binder down on the bed with Bast. The first object was a black orb. It appeared to be obsidian and even though she didn't know why, she felt drawn to it. She picked it up and held it. She could feel its energy and power. There was definitely something special about her connection to this stone, and she would have to figure out what that was.

The next object on the dresser was a knife. She took it out of the leather sheath. It was a beautiful knife. The handle looked as though it was a curling serpent and the hilt had a wing-like design on it. The blade came out of the snake's mouth. It was beautiful and somehow fitting. *A symbol of freedom and free will.* She placed it carefully back in its sheath.

She sat it back down and noticed next to it lay a deck of tarot cards and an obsidian pendulum. *Obsidian? Hmmm. This seems to be a pattern. Who is leaving these gifts? And how do they know so much about me?*

As she moved closer, her foot hit something and as she looked down, she saw an Ouija board sitting on the ground beside the dresser. She picked it up and looked at it. *Hmmm. This might prove useful.* She sat it down inside the dresser for now. There would be time for that later.

She decided it was time to start her reading in these binders. As she turned to the bed, she saw a black leather bag on the pillow with a note. She picked up the note and read it:

Hello, Eira

> *Here is a little gift I thought you might like. It might help you carry around the items you have acquired. Oh, and don't worry, this is a special bag. It can hold more than you think. You won't run out of space. I thought you might like the simplicity and style of the bag. It suits you.*
> *Your friend,*
> *MC*

MC? Who was MC? Was it Miss Cameron? If so, she might know more than she is letting on. Eira turned her attention to the bag. It was black leather, and it looked like a big pocket on a strap, but something about the simplicity of that made Eira happy. It was closed with a crystal button. It was white and Eira couldn't place what the stone was called, but it was familiar. She stuck the smaller objects on the nightstand inside it, along with the cat she had received from Mastema.

She then sat down on her spot on the bed to read. She had a feeling she might be in here a while. The binders were big and overflowing. She sighed and picked up the first one…

Chapter 8: Midnight

She sat there quietly reading until she reached the last sentence, but in the middle of her reading, the book was snatched from her. Eira looked up, angry someone would disturb her in such a way. She calmed down once she realized it was Miss Cameron. She sighed. She knew this was inevitable.

"Ello, Miss Cameron. How are you today?"

"Eira, do you know what time it is?"

Eira glanced outside. The sun was setting. She turned back to Miss Cameron. "Probably close to dinner time, I would say."

Miss Cameron sighed. "Yes, my dear. That is correct. Have you any idea how long you have been in here?"

Eira thought about it a moment. "Judging by the face you are making, Miss Cameron, I am going to say longer than three days?"

Miss Cameron was obviously annoyed. "It has been a week, my dear. You are going to waste away if you don't start eating more regularly."

"I will be fine. I don't really need all that much food."

"It isn't good for you to sit in this dark room all the time either. And reading in such low light is bad for your eyes."

"I find the darkness comforting and I can see better in it."

Miss Cameron sighed. It was obvious she would not get anywhere with the child. So, she moved toward the door. "I will see you at dinner or I will drag you down."

"Do you insist everyone here eats as much as you do me?"

Miss Cameron did not answer. She simply closed the door.

The next day Eira went on a search for Midnight's room. She had taken off again when Eira had tried to approach her the night before at dinner. She didn't seem to like her. Eira couldn't figure out why. Maybe it was because she was so much older than the other inmates? No. That wouldn't make sense. She seemed to like Eden just fine. But didn't Mastema say they showed up together? Eden seemed to be Eira's age. Were they possibly related? Oh well, she would figure out what her problem was today. She heard Mastema's voice. *Be careful.* Be careful? Of what, she wondered. Eira shook her head and decided she had better proceed. She knocked on the door three times.

Midnight opened the door and stared down at her. "What do you want?"

"To talk to you."

Midnight folded her arms and glared down at her, obviously annoyed. "And what makes you think I want to talk to you?"

"I don't. I know you don't particularly like me, but I have spoken with Eden's Promise and like I told her, we live together now, so we might as well be civil."

Midnight grunted and moved from the door. "Fine. But don't stay long."

Eira didn't move. Midnight glared at her, obviously annoyed. "Well? Aren't you going to come in?"

Eira shifted nervously. " Um…I…well, I have to be invited."

Midnight grunted. "Figures. I should have known." Midnight walked further into the room. She stopped with her back to Eira. She was silent for a minute, then she turned around, throwing her arms out to her sides. "Well, Miss Candles, would you please come in?"

Eira nodded and entered the room. There was a bed with a doll sitting on it. Beside the bed, she had a dresser and on the other side of the room was a table in front of a mirror. This one was much smaller than Mastema's. Beside it was a shelf. Eira surveyed the room. The mirror seemed to have an array of photos of a young boy and a random letter in an envelope. The envelope had some perfume on it.

Eira stared at it for a long time until Midnight got in front of her. "What are you looking at, brat?"

Eira glared at her. *I am not a brat.* "I was just wondering who the boy was and if he was the one the letter was for."

"That is none of your business!" Midnight snapped.

"No, but I would like to get to know you."

Silence. The two girls stared at each other. Waiting. Eira half expected Midnight to ask her to leave when she said, "His name was Stephan. He was a childhood friend. When I was first dropped off here, he had just escaped the facility that he came from. He was different…nice…charming. We grew up here together for a while. We were in love or at least that is what I thought. Then one day, we had snuck out against Miss Cameron's wishes. We went out past the gate and people from Project Damen found us. They were going to drag us both back to it, but he told me to run. I did. That was the last I saw of him. That letter showed up the day you arrived. It says it is from him and it is scented with my favorite perfume."

"Do you think it is really from him?"

"I don't know."

Midnight played with a crystal necklace around her neck. Eira didn't look at her but said, "That is a pretty necklace."

Midnight seemed lost in thought and absently replied, "Yes, it was the last thing my mother gave me before she died."

"My condolences for your loss."

When Midnight didn't respond, Eira decided it was best to change the subject for now and walked over to the shelf where she saw some tarot cards, some books, a game of checkers, and a pendulum. *Some of this stuff is similar to what I found in my room. Could she be the one sending the gifts instead of Miss Cameron? Doubtful...what reason would she have?* Eira picked up the checkerboard. "Do you play?"

"No...not anymore."

Midnight sat on her bed and picked up a book, obviously intent on ignoring the girl and her conversation. Eira sighed and moved closer to her. Initially, she was determined to get her to play with her. Then she decided while she was distracted, she could take a closer look the boy. He looked familiar. Eira stared at the images. The boy looked familiar. She knew that face. He looked like her brother. *Impossible.* She dropped the checkerboard and its parts, the pieces scattering on the floor.

Midnight jumped up from her bed. "What the hell? What is wrong with you?"

Eira didn't move. She kept staring at the photo. Midnight crossed the room and grabbed her, spinning her around. "I said, what the hell is wrong with you?"

Eira pointed at the pictures. "...my brother..."

Midnight looked at the photos and then back at Eira. "Your brother? Doubtful. I thought your brother was closer to your age?"

Eira looked at her startled. "Last time I saw him, he would have been about my age now...but how would you know that?"

"Nothing around here is a secret. The walls have eyes and ears. The wind tells all secrets. So how old was your brother before he disappeared?"

"I don't know…"

"What do you mean you don't know?" Midnight crossed her arms, obviously annoyed.

"I don't even know how old I am…"

Eira looked down at the ground. There was a strange emotion she was feeling, but what was it? It felt like a loss. Midnight watched her for a minute. "Oh, geez. Are you going to cry, brat?"

"No…I don't cry…"

"I don't have time for this. Get out."

Eira didn't move. Midnight grabbed her arm and dragged her to the door and threw her out it. "I SAID GET OUT!"

Eira sat on the ground, bewildered and confused for a minute. Why didn't she know how old her brother was? Why didn't she know her own age? At the facility, there was no way to know the time or the days that passed. No one told her about her birthday or how long she had been there. It was an endless span of time. Was that boy in the pictures really her brother? If so, how long had he been gone? What happened to him? Why hadn't he come back for her?

Midnight sat in silence at her desk. Checkers were scattered all over her floor, but she didn't care. She stared at the letter he had left.

My dearest Midnight,

> *I hope this letter finds you in good spirits. I know it has been years since we last saw each other, but you are still my heart. I am sorry I dragged you into my failed attempt to rescue my sister. Had I known that you would be harmed, I would have done it on my own. I hope you can forgive me for leaving you like I did. I am glad, however, to know that you did get away. All these years back at home, I was always scared that they had gotten you too. I had to check, so I released everyone in the facility looking for you. Luckily, my sister has led us back together. Please give her the photo inside and help bring her to me so she and I can end this whole mess before it begins.*

> *Your forever love,*

> *Stephan.*

Midnight sat there quietly. Could this really be the sister they had snuck out to save all those years ago? *I thought she was older than this.* Suddenly, Midnight heard Mastema chime in. *That is because she is. Remember, things aren't always as they appear outwardly.* Midnight chuckled. She hated when Mastema invaded her privacy like this, but perhaps she was right. Well, what did he mean they need to end this mess before it begins? What mess could he be talking about.

Midnight walked over to the door and peered out to see if Eira was still there. The girl was gone. She was sure good at disappearing…like someone else she used to know. She sighed. *I will probably have to go find her.*

Eira had returned to her room. This time there were no gifts when she got there. She sat down on the bed. She was so confused. How long had she been in there? How long had her brother been gone? It had felt like ages but was it really? Meeting

Midnight made her believe so. When she had inquired to Miss Cameron about her age, Miss Cameron hadn't known but harbored a guess at around the age of eight, but now she was questioning if that was true.

Eira didn't like being confused and unsure. It was uncomfortable, but so was any other emotion. She didn't like feeling this way. It made her angry, but at least anger was something she understood. It was comfortable.

Suddenly there was a knock at the door. Eira stood up and stared at the door. Then suddenly, it opened slightly, and something slid in. She went over to the door and peered out it, but whoever it was had vanished. She picked up the object. It was a book with a letter attached to it. The book was on Astrology and Star Signs. She opened the letter. Inside was a small note:

I am sorry for how I treated you. Take this. It belongs to you.

No one had signed it, so who was it from? Midnight? She pulled out a picture from inside the envelope. It was a picture of patient 42. Why would Midnight give her a picture of him? She turned it over and there was a message written on the back:

Hello,

> *It has been a while, little sister. But don't worry. I am coming for you. We will finish this story before it begins. You will be mine again.*
>
> *Love Your Dearest Brother,*
>
> *S.*

She stared at the note. She didn't even realize she had dropped the book. She kept staring at the note. Was it really from her brother? If so, what did he mean by this? And why did it fill her with a sense of ominous dread?

She knelt down and picked up the book and laid it with the picture on the desk. She sat down on the bed. She sat there in silence for a while, staring at her lap. She didn't want to believe that Patient 42 was her brother. She hadn't had much experience with him but what she had heard, experienced, and felt at his door meant that he wasn't the same person she had grown up with. Could she have been lied to all this time? If that was her brother, was all her good memories a lie? Could she even trust herself? Her own memory? What if everything she knew was a lie? Was her whole experience just something fabricated in her head? Was someone changing and manipulating her memory? What purpose would they have? Or was it true? If it was true, what did they do to change her brother?

Eira sat in silence, wanting to be angry but not being able to. She was filled with this deep sadness. She clenched her fists on her lap as the tears formed in her eyes. She tried to swipe them away. *What is this? Tears? I don't cry. I never cry. Crying is a weakness and I refuse to be weak.* But she couldn't stop. She tried to be angry, but she didn't have the energy. She picked up the picture and the book and threw it. But the tears just wouldn't stop. *What is wrong with me?*

Mastema felt like telling her that nothing was wrong with her but knew now wasn't the time. Eira would need to figure out her own path, and right now, she wasn't willing to accept the reality before her. She simply wasn't willing to come into the truth yet.

Eira, feeling defeated by this strange emotion, decided it would be best to go to sleep. She curled up on the bed and waited till the emotion and tears exhausted her into sleep.

Chapter 9: Miss Cameron

When Eira woke up, she still wasn't feeling any better about her situation. However, she came to accept that the person she once knew as her brother was no longer the same person. She didn't know what had made him go so crazy or bad, but she had a feeling that if she hadn't escaped when she did, they would have warped her the same way. Almost everyone there either went down a dark path or died in the process.

However, despite accepting the reality, she was not yet ready to meet anyone else or deal with any more knowledge that they might bring. So, in that respect, Eira decided she would stay in her room till she regained control of her emotions and came to terms with the loss of her brother. It would be unacceptable for anyone to see her this way. However, she knew would have to leave to go to meals. That way, Miss Cameron wouldn't worry. After all, she had no way of knowing how long it would take her to come to terms with her new reality. Maybe she would even try reading that new book.

Miss Cameron was worried about Eira. Aside from meals, she was spending a lot of time in her room. She could tell that Eira was going through something, but she was unsure of what. This had been going on for a few weeks, so Miss Cameron decided she should check in on her. Miss Cameron knocked on her door. Eira didn't answer. Miss Cameron knocked again. Still nothing. She called out her name but nothing. Well, this was certainly concerning.

She opened the door, expecting to see Eira sitting upright and meditating on her bed like she usually was. This time though, Eira was sitting in the corner, curled up in a ball in the corner, which was unusual for the girl. Miss Cameron entered cautiously. "Eira?"

Eira didn't move or look up. She was still. Miss Cameron approached the bed. She sat down on the bed. She waited. When Eira didn't move for a while or seem to acknowledge her, Miss Cameron reached for her. She placed her hand on her arm, which rested on her knee. When she did, she could feel Eira flinch and tense up. She moved her hand a bit to get her to look up, but it only made Eira tense more. Miss Cameron decided it was best to leave her be for now and removed her hand. Eira still didn't look up, so Miss Cameron got up. "I am here for you, Eira. If you need me, please come find me."

Miss Cameron moved to go to the door. She was about to reach for the door handle when suddenly Eira spoke. "Miss Cameron?"

Miss Cameron turned around. Eira was staring at her. There were tears on her face. Something Miss Cameron never expected to see from the girl. Perhaps they hadn't broken her. Perhaps there was still hope that she would still choose her own path. Miss Cameron looked at her and smiled. "Yes, my dear."

"What happened to my brother? How could he become this monster?"

"Well, dear, sometimes bad things happen to good people, and the good person inside cannot handle it, and sometimes they break and, in an attempt to survive, become just as bad as the evil that was enacted on them."

"But how? He wasn't...He couldn't..."

Miss Cameron sat back down on the bed. "Your brother came here when he was young, He talked about you a lot and was hell-bent on rescuing you. I warned him about leaving the safety of The Asylum. He didn't listen and he left to go rescue you, and they found him. They took him back and I can only imagine what happened to him when he returned. He was the first success of the facility you grew up in."

"Why is it we are safe here, anyway? How do you keep us safe?"

"That is complicated to explain, but the gist is that the humans in the village who were hunting you are in one realm of existence. The facility you were in and the other facility, while there are people from other realms running them, they also have a lot of human people there helping them. The Asylum exists in another realm and only incredibly special beings can cross into this realm or find it. We are kind of in between, so to speak. Makes it hard to find us or access The Asylum without the proper training. Besides, the facilities and The Asylum have a long-standing agreement from before I was in charge that we all still honor. After all, who are we without our word?"

"But someone did find it...that first day I got here."

"Yes. One of our own did come searching for you. However, there are certain rules that must be followed. And we have an arrangement."

"Rules? Arrangements? What are you talking about?"

"I cannot tell you."

"Why not?"

"You will know when it is important for you to know."

Eira was obviously displeased with this response.

After some silence, Miss Cameron asked. "How long are you going to isolate yourself?"

"I don't know. I will come out when I am ready. I promise."

Miss Cameron sighed. "You know where to find me."

Miss Cameron got up to leave again. This time when Eira spoke, she did not turn around.

"What is the purpose of these facilities?"

"To create hybrids…"

"Hybrids? Hybrids of what?"

"The demonic and the angelic, my dear."

"I don't understand…"

"You have read *The Bible*, correct?"

"Yes…but I—"

"Well, then you should have a basic understanding of angels and demons…or at least how humans perceive things. After all, the concepts of angels and demons is largely a human construct. Humans see angels as beings of light and harbingers of God. They are the source of good. Whereas demons are seen as beings of darkness and servants of the devil who only bring chaos and evil. However, sometimes things aren't always as they appear and good intentions can lead someone down a bad path…which can lead to their demonification. However, the world has a balance and there is no one true source of good and evil."

Eira was silent as if contemplating the information Miss Cameron had told her. Miss Cameron studied her carefully. She had read the book and yet she still seemed confused by the notion that God may not necessarily be all good.

She waited a moment and then continued. "God is considered to be all things by the humans. In this sense, he is both good and evil. That is just how it is. Now I believe that when God created the world, he intended for the good of people and for good to be triumphant in the world. However, free will is a tricky thing. People may have been made from a perfect being, but they themselves are far from perfect…and therefore, people make mistakes. They do bad things. That does not make them bad, just as doing good things does not make them good. Their choices are

64

good and bad, but they just are. In this sense, God also created angels and, by extension, demons. Unfortunately, many beings like ourselves tend to buy into this view of things and align themselves with how the humans would perceive them instead of choosing for themselves. But everything has a balance and therefore has potential for great good or great evil just like God Himself."

"What are you saying, Miss Cameron?"

"Well, if you are to believe what the humans teach, there was a fall. And if we are to believe this then even their "angels" have free will and the ability to make poor choices. Therefore, they have great potential for good and evil and therefore, so do what they call "demons". Humans like things to stay black and white. They don't like gray areas, and they like having someone to rely on when in trouble…and someone to blame for their trouble. Unfortunately, beings like you and I got the short end of the stick. However, we can still choose how we will be. You do not have to be what they believe you to be, my dear."

Eira was silent for a long time. This idea that she had a choice was still new to her. She could be the monster they had designed her to be. Or to be something better. She was quiet so long that Miss Cameron had begun to think that their conversation was over, but before she could turn away, Eira spoke. "What am I, then?"

"Well, my dear, that is complicated. You see, their experiments had always failed when they tried to do it within one child. Your brother was their first success, but what purpose he served in turning him into what he has become, I do not know the end goal. After a few more failures, they discovered that it was a lot more stable if they split the energy and power between two children. Twins…"

"So, does that mean I have a twin?"

"Yes, my dear. She was at the other facility with your parents. We do not know if any of them survived."

Eira was silent. Eira had so many questions she wanted to ask, but she wasn't sure if now was the time or even where to start. Miss Cameron opened the door. As she stepped outside, Eira had to ask one final question. "Is there any hope for my brother?"

"There is always hope. Remember hope is the denial of reality, but without it all is lost."

With that, the door closed.

A few more weeks had gone by. Mastema worried that Eira would never leave her room, so she reached out. *Hello, Eira. How are we doing today?*

"Hello, Mastema."

You seem upset.

Eira remained silent.

Tell me what is wrong. It isn't like anyone else is around to overhear us talking. Worst case is someone thinks you are talking to yourself, right?

Eira sighed. "I just don't know anything anymore. I feel like everything I know is a lie. Apparently, my brother has become a monster and I have a twin. I feel like everything I know and believe has all been an illusion and a lie."

Well, that can be distressing.

"Do you have any idea how it feels to question your memory and what you believe? To question if any of it was real or all fabricated and just placed inside your mind by someone else? How am I supposed to move forward and trust myself if I don't even know if I can trust my own memory? I feel like I am going crazy."

Well, if you are going crazy, at least you are already in an asylum.

Eira grunted. She obviously was not amused.

We are all a little crazy. That's what makes life fun. However, I can assure you that you are not going crazy. We all see the world through our own perceptions...our own mind's eye. We interpret what is happening around and to us in our own unique ways. If you took a hundred people and subjected them to the same situation and circumstance, each one would respond differently and handle the aftermath differently. They would all recover at different speeds, and they would all remember it differently, even if it was the exact same every single time. So, can you trust your memory? No. But it is all you have. The way your unique mind remembers your unique experiences is special to you.

Silence.

No. Your memories aren't lies. They are the truth. Your truth. Everyone lives their own truth. What happened to you and everyone else here is unforgivable, but we must move forward. If we are going to find THE truth and get you back to where you belong, we need to focus. Your brother can wait. I have a feeling that you two will be reunited before you know it.

Silence.

Look outside.

Eira turned to look out the window. There was a strange white substance falling from the sky and it seemed to cover the ground and trees outside.

"What is it?"

Snow.

Eira had never seen snow before. It was strange and made everything seem so bright outside even though the sky was darker. Eira smiled. This strange new thing made her feel peaceful, but she didn't know why. Suddenly her door came open. Eira glanced at Miss Cameron.

Miss Cameron smiled at her. "Would you like to go outside, Eira?"

Eira nodded. Miss Cameron led her outside. Eira stepped in the snow and noticed she was leaving footprints. This was exciting. Although she didn't know why and couldn't explain why she felt the sudden urge to destroy all the new spotless snow with footprints. Suddenly Eira was hit with something cold. She turned around and Miss Cameron was there, holding what appeared to be a ball of snow.

"Hey! What is…"

Eira was hit with another snowball.

"It is a snowball, my dear. Wanna play?"

Eira didn't know what a snowball was. But wait…where was everyone else?

Miss Cameron smiled at her as if knowing what she was thinking about. "Don't worry about it, dear. They will come out when they are ready. Until then, why don't you and I have a little fun."

Eira smiled. She didn't know what a snowball was or how to construct one, but it couldn't be that hard. She picked up a handful of snow and tried, but it failed. She kept trying but quickly grew frustrated. Miss Cameron chuckled and approached Eira. "Here, let me show you." Miss Cameron scooped up some snow in each hand. "First, you scoop up snow in each hand, like this."

Eira did the same. Miss Cameron then brought her hands together. "Now, you will want to bring your hands together and kind of rotate them like this, slowly increasing the pressure. See?"

Miss Cameron held out the newly formed snowball and Eira tried again. Miss Cameron could see she was still struggling, so she knelt down beside her and put her hands over hers and helped her with the motion. Eira was a little shocked by this and didn't know what to think. It was strangely nice having Miss Cameron around like this. It filled Eira with an emotion she was unfamiliar with, but it made her feel warm inside. When Miss Cameron removed her hands, Eira was holding a snowball. Miss Cameron smiled. "Now try again."

This time Eira did it by herself. Eira smiled. Miss Cameron stared at her for a while, watching her admire the snowball. It was nice to see the child smile. A genuine smile. Not one caused by pain...but by joy. Miss Cameron stood up. "Shall we begin?"

Eira nodded.

Eira got so involved with the snowball fight that she hadn't noticed the other inmates had joined them outside. This was a peculiar thing for her...to be having fun without someone else getting hurt. Eira stopped and noticed the other children had built a hill of snow and were sliding down it. She didn't understand why they thought such a silly thing was fun. Miss Cameron asked if she wanted to join. Eira declined. Instead, she chose Miss Cameron to show her how to make more things out of snow.

Miss Cameron agreed and helped Eira make a snowman. She even helped her decorate him with his own rock buttons, twig arms, carrot nose, coal eyes, and a scarf and hat. Eira even put gloves on the twig arms so his hands wouldn't get cold. Miss Cameron was delighted to see that there was still somewhat of a child in her and that there was a caring side to her.

When they were done, she noticed one of the other inmates was not there. Mastema was not there. She looked back at the Asylum, and in one window, she could see Mastema looking out. She wondered why she was up there watching instead of joining them, but before she could question it, Miss Cameron grabbed her from behind and began tickling her and spinning her around. Eira resisted causing both to fall to the ground, laughing.

Suddenly Miss Cameron rolled away and moved her arms and legs in the snow. Eira looked at her, confused. Miss Cameron laughed. "I am making a snow angel. Come on, give it a try."

Eira moved her arms and legs like Miss Cameron was then they both stood up. Eira could see the outline of an angel in the snow for both. Miss Cameron's was obviously bigger and appeared to have some pointed ears. Eira looked at Miss Cameron quizzically. Miss Cameron smiled and put her finger to her lip as if telling Eira to be quiet. Eira didn't understand, but she couldn't help but smile. Miss Cameron was definitely an angel. She was so nice and wonderful. This was the closest Eira had ever been to having a mom. Eira felt bad thinking that though. It felt as though it was a betrayal to the mother she had never met.

Eira turned and looked at the snow angel she had made. At first, it made her smile. But then, suddenly, her expression grew darker. Miss Cameron watched her, concerned. "Eira, what's wrong?"

Eira didn't respond. She kept staring at it. Today had been so perfect. She didn't want it to be ruined, but how could things be so beautiful here in this moment when everything else about her feels shrouded in darkness. Eira clenched her fists. Tears were coming down her face again. *Why am I becoming so weak?* As if sensing her struggle Miss Cameron got down beside her. She grabbed her shoulders and turned Eira towards her. Eira wouldn't look up. She didn't want Miss Cameron to see her this way. Miss Cameron gently asked again, "What is wrong, my dear?"

Silence. Miss Cameron waited. Eventually, Eira broke her silence. "I just don't understand…"

"Understand what, my dear?"

"Why everything is so nice here…why you are so nice to me…why you care so much about me. I don't understand how this world can be so beautiful and yet so full of darkness. I don't understand why I cannot be good…" Eira kicked snow over her snow angel. "Angels are perfect and good…and pure. I am none of those things…I am evil. Why am I evil, Miss Cameron? Why was I made a demon? And why do you care so much about me…when you are so wonderful…"

Miss Cameron was silent for a moment but then said, "Things are nice here because everyone deserves some niceness in their life. I am nice to you because everyone needs someone in their life who will be kind to them and never give up on them. Everyone here is like family to me, but you are my family. And I love you. You are not evil, my dear. You haven't chosen your path yet. I see much good in you, dearie."

Eira remained silent. Miss Cameron continued. "This world we live in has both good and evil in it. Everything has the potential for both. Unfortunately, people tend to lean toward the darkness, but there is good and beauty in the world. Nature will always balance itself. You have good in you, too. Demon or not. Angels aren't that perfect either. Just like everyone else, they have the potential for great good and great evil…what is different is the path they choose, my dear. You can still choose your path. You do not have to be what they made you to be. You have a choice."

Eira looked up at Miss Cameron, tears still streaming her face. She wanted so desperately to believe her, but how could she? Miss Cameron wrapped her in a hug and then carried her inside. She gave her some cocoa, and then they went to her room. Miss Cameron had Eira lay down in the bed, and she sat on the edge of the bed. Eira watched Miss Cameron closely before asking, "What did you mean, I am your family?"

Miss Cameron took in a deep breath. "Everyone here is like family to me, Eira. But you are different."

"Different how, Miss Cameron?"

71

Miss Cameron turned toward the door. She knew she would have to tell the girl and that lying was not an option. She wanted to deflect the question but knew it would be better to tell her. She didn't want her to think she was lying or keeping things from her. She would never gain her trust then.

"Your mother is my twin sister. You see, this Asylum was the beginning of the facilities. Where the humans first began their tests. They were unsuccessful using only one child as one side would survive or they wouldn't survive at all, but twins worked. Me and your mother were the first pair of twins they managed to create. We survived together. We were close. But then, when we were about your age, someone else took over the project, and they had more nefarious plans for the Asylum. Her and I were separated. One day I found her and when I saw what they were doing to her I lost it…the survivors fled. The project was closed down for some time after that. Then as we got older and discovered for ourselves what we were capable of, she decided she wanted to go where we belonged, but I didn't feel I belonged with the others, so I let her go. Ironically, your mother, despite her angelic nature, fell for someone a lot darker, your father. He hooked up with another band of humans to try again. But this time to make them more pure…less human. However, I don't think he has completely abandoned the idea of using humans as pawns. Everything was fine at first, even after your brother was born, but then after the union that brought you and your sister into existence, something went wrong with your mother. So, your father cut ties with the humans and created a new facility. One ran by your mother to take in the angelic ones and even the demonic ones who wanted to do better and be better to help them to their full potential for good. However, when he fled, he was only able to take your mother, who was clinging to your sister at the time. You and your brother were left behind."

72

"Wait…then why are you here? Why didn't he come back for us?"

"I stayed here because I didn't feel like I belonged with the others after all. I am not angelic and I am not evil either. As for why he didn't come back for you…I don't know. I knew the facility was crumbling, and you were healthy, so they had moved you into another room. When the facility began to incinerate, he got your mother and sister out, but he didn't think you or your brother had survived the facility's collapse. Your mother was in poor health, so he took her away. He said he was going to go back to look, but he never did. Instead, the humans rebuilt their facility and kept you and your brother and the rest of the survivors for their own nefarious purposes. After all, humans do create the best monsters."

"Do you not like humans?"

"That is complicated, my dear."

Eira didn't know how to process this information or what to do. She knew she should have thousands of questions, but she could not think of any. Silence filled the room. Miss Cameron suddenly turned and looked at her with a smile. "How about a bedtime story, dear?"

Eira nodded.

Miss Cameron began. "Once upon a time…"

As she spoke, Eira drifted off into sleep.

Chapter 10: Kas

When Eira awoke, Miss Cameron was gone. Eira was a little upset that Miss Cameron hadn't informed her of their relation beforehand, but at least now she understood why she felt so close to Miss Cameron. Miss Cameron was not only her aunt, but they were the same. Miss Cameron could understand her in a way she didn't think her parents would be able to. Well, it was time to stop isolating herself in her room and finish the task Miss Cameron had given her of talking to the other inmates. The next inmate on the list was Kas.

Eira went to her door and knocked. Kas invited her to come inside. Her room had a lot of Egyptian décor, including Hieroglyphic writing on the walls and statues of various Egyptian Gods. Eira even noticed one in particular of Anubis standing beside a crystal pyramid. Kas was sitting on the floor, messing with something that Eira could not see. Without looking at her, Kas said, "I see you have Bastet with you."

"Bastet?"

"The cat."

Eira reached into her pouch and pulled out the stuffed cat that Mastema had given her. "You mean this?"

Kas didn't turn around but nodded. "Bastet is a good ally. I would like to give you another."

Kas stood up and walked toward Eira. She grabbed Eira's hand and placed her hand over hers. She then removed her hand and there was a statue of Anubis. Eira didn't know how she had transported this statue to her without her seeing. Yes, it wasn't a big statue but should have been noticeable. It was roughly the same size as the cat she had received from Mastema.

Kas then turned away. "Anubis will help you along your journey. You will find the truth that you seek, child. Now go."

Eira was confused by Kas' behavior but decided it was best not to upset her and left with the new addition to her collection. She placed both back in her pouch and started back to her room. As she walked back to her room, one of the other inmates banged on the door to their room. It had startled her, causing her to jump back. The door said Mas Rami. Eira approached the door. "Mas?"

"Who are you? Go away."

"I am Eira. Why are you banging on your door?"

"I want the voices to stop…please go away…" Another loud bang

"The voices?"

"Yes, the voices like you! They never stop talking. I just want out. I just want to find the truth. I want to know the truth. But these voices won't stop. They won't leave me alone." A few more loud bangs

"You are going to hurt yourself."

"I said go away! Stop talking! You are just another voice in my head…"

Eira was about to open the door to calm the person on the other side when Miss Cameron grabbed her arm. "Mas, you are ok, dear. You need to settle down now and take a nap."

The banging stopped. Miss Cameron turned toward Eira and they walked away. "What was that about, Miss Cameron?"

"Mas was at the second facility. They dropped her off here though. They said something happened at the facility that seemed to break her and another inmate we have here, a Maddy Hellfire. They were both dropped off here. Mas constantly talks about needing to find the truth about something and the voices in her head. She doesn't seem to have any memory of how she got here or much anything else. I cannot figure out what she is going on about or what she is seeking answers to. It is concerning…"

"And what about Maddy?"

"Oh, Maddy? She hears voices too. Her voices mostly tell her to stay even though every time I have spoken with her, she wants to leave. Every time she tries, the voices go crazy and drive her crazy, so she remains here."

"Where does she want to go?"

"I don't know. I think she just doesn't want to be in any facility. Just wants to be free with the humans."

"Isn't that dangerous, Miss Cameron?"

"Yes, it is…"

"Why do you think she wants to go there, then?"

"I don't know."

"Perhaps the two issues are related…"

"Perhaps, my dear. Perhaps…"

Miss Cameron escorted Eira back to her room. When they arrived Eira opened the door but before entering, said, "Miss Cameron?"

"Yes, dear?"

"I thought the second facility was supposed to be better than the one I came from…"

"It is…"

"Then why do they seemingly abandon their children here? None of them seems to be doing any better than the ones from the facility I came from.. And Mas and Maddy…"

Silence.

"I do not know what happens at the facilities if that is what you want to know. I do not know why they drop them off here or why they are so broken when they arrive. What happened to them is a mystery. All I can do is try to help until they feel able to share with me."

" I just do not understand..."

She still had her back to Miss Cameron, but Miss Cameron could tell by her voice she was filled with sadness. "Understand what, my dear?"

"You said my mother was angelic and good and that my father was darker. But if they are doing this to people..."

"Eira," Miss Cameron interrupted. "I do know that whatever happened to these people here was done to them without your mother's knowledge."

Eira remained silent.

"Your father initially set it up with good intentions. Your mother had changed him in a way I didn't believe possible...but old habits are hard to break."

Still silence.

"Eira, you are not evil."

Eira entered the room and closed the door. As she did, she turned slightly and Miss Cameron saw that she had tears on her face.

Chapter 11: Pheonix

After Eira had talked to Miss Cameron, she decided it would be best to leave Mas and Maddy to themselves for now. Most of what they said sounded like ramblings of truly crazy people and while Eira was messed up, she didn't think she was crazy enough to make sense of what they were trying to tell her. So here she was outside the door of an inmate she wasn't sure she had seen before named Phoenix. Phoenix opened the door and invited her in without being prompted for the invite. She simply explained that oddities like that traveled quickly through the inmates.

When Eira entered, the first thing she became aware of was the empty bird cage standing in the center of the room. She stared at it for a moment wondering why she would have a bird cage. She also noted the fact Phoenix had no bed. She wanted to question it, but before she could, Phoenix said, "The bird cage is symbolic to me. It is a part of who I am."

Symbolic? Of what, I wonder? After a moment, Eira asked, "Where do you sleep?"

"In the cage…"

"Why would you want to sleep in a cage?"

"You wouldn't understand…"

"Try me?"

Phoenix said nothing for a while. Eira kept looking around. She had similar things in the room to the other inmates. A pendulum. Some tarot cards. Runes. The main difference was she had an old-looking tea set. Eira had about given up that Phoenix would explain the cage, but then she spoke. "We are all caged. Caged birds unable to fly free. One day we will have to be set free and be allowed to see if we live or die. Without leaving what binds

78

us behind, we cannot move forward. However, not everyone is strong enough for that journey and many of us are probably going to die."

"What do you mean many of us are going to die?"

"The inmates…"

"Why would you think that?"

"I saw it in my vision…"

"Your vision?"

"Yes. The Higher Powers give me messages. I only deliver them."

"And what did your vision foretell?"

"That soon this place will come under attack from the humans and the dark souls they are in allegiance with. We will have to choose to fight or flee. Whichever we choose will bring much death. And I have a feeling something is waiting…"

"What is waiting? And what is it waiting for?"

"I do not know what it is, but I believe it is waiting for you…"

Eira felt unsettled by this but figured she would not get a less vague answer, so instead she asked, "You said no matter what we do, there will be much death. So, it does not matter what we do when this assault comes?"

"No…it does not matter. The outcome is the same. Just different lives are taken."

"Are your visions usually correct?"

"Always…"

"Always? Don't you think that is a bit overconfident?"

"No…because I have never been wrong…"

Eira didn't know what to make of this. Miss Cameron had mentioned there was an inmate was good at prophecies and had visions but was this the person she was talking about? And if it was, what did that mean for the future? What was waiting for her?

"What is waiting for me?"

"I do not know…"

"I thought you said you had a vision?"

"I did. I had two visions. One showing each choice and its corresponding outcome."

"Hmm."

"What?"

"Your higher power must not know everything if it has to give you multiple visions."

"Well, the higher power has designs within designs, but we do have free will and there is always more than one possible outcome. The scenario in which the place comes under attack is what they are warning me about. Apparently, that has become a reality or, rather, will become a reality in the near future. As such, the higher power needed to warn me. Problem is with free will, there are different scenarios based on the decisions made by everyone in the present moment."

"Then how come you only got two visions instead of many? Any little choice made by anyone in either scenario could change the outcome even if just in a small way."

"Yes…you are right. However, I feel the higher power sends me the two most likely outcomes based on the information of each person in the scenario and their tendencies. The main difference between the two most likely outcomes is one choice made."

"And who makes that choice?"

"Miss Cameron, of course."

"Have you told her about your vision?"

"Yes…"

Eira waited for a moment to see if Phoenix would finish her thought. After a bit, she finally did. "I told her that we were going to be attacked and she would need to decide if we would fight or flee and depending on her choice, many would die."

"Did you tell her who would die?"

"No…"

"Why not?"

"Because it is not an easy decision to choose who will live and who will die. Especially not if you love and care for all parties involved. It is not a decision I wish to place on the poor dear. This way, she can make her decision with a clean conscience."

"I see…you didn't answer my earlier question. What is out to get me?"

"I told you I do not know…"

"Yes, but as I said, you had a *vision* and that indicates that you should know what is coming for me…"

"Well, I couldn't tell exactly what it was, but it looked like a shrouded figure and there was a distinct sensation of pure evil coming from it."

Sounds like patient 42…my brother…

Eira decided it was time to leave. She was curious as to when this attack would take place but didn't figure that information would be given in the vision and she was even more curious to see which way Miss Cameron leaned in her decision. However, if

81

she wanted to go meet the other two inmates before the night ended, she would have to leave. She approached the door and then stopped.

"This evil that is after me...does it get me?"

"Yes..."

"No matter what the outcome?"

"Yes..."

"Will I die?"

"Yes and no..."

"Yes and no? Either I die or I don't. Which is it?"

"It is complicated. You will have to decide for yourself one day."

Eira let out a frustrated growl and left. She should have known better than to expect a straight answer from Phoenix. Seemed like the girl lived in a world of vagueness and it was irritating. How could someone answer a question and not answer it at the same time anyway. She decided to clear her mind of it and go back to her room. The twins could wait till the morning. After that headache. She needed a rest.

It didn't occur to her until she got to her room Phoenix was the first person to not give her something when she left. This was also the first time there was nothing waiting in her room when she got back. That was fine with her, though. She didn't need any more riddles from Phoenix to solve.

Chapter 12: The Twins

Eira woke up and began her search for Lily Hallow and Marie Dipper. In all her days of wandering the halls, she didn't recall seeing their rooms, but Miss Cameron had assured her they were in the room between Mas Rami and Maddy Hellfire. Eira had found her way back to that hallway and stood outside a door labeled Lily Hallow and Mary Dipper. These two were the only two inmates who shared a room and when Eira had inquired as to why Miss Cameron had only said that they had determined it would be best not to separate them.

Eira knocked on the door and waited, but there was no response. She knocked again. Still no answer. She tried one more time. "Hello?"

She could hear movement on the inside, but no one answered her. Eira sighed and considered leaving it be, but then she remembered Miss Cameron telling her she may have to be persistent. She pushed on the door to see if it was locked. It wasn't. The door swung open. There were two girls. One sat on the bed, reading a book and holding a stuffed cat. She had long blond hair, which majorly contrasted with her dark skin. Something about her felt unnatural. She could see her peering over the book she was reading, and her rainbow eyes seemed to pierce through Eira's soul. Eira suddenly felt very self-conscious and averted her gaze.

She turned her attention to the other girl lying on her bed, playing with a knife while staring at what appeared to be a rock. She had long white hair matching her snow-white skin. She, too, turned to look at Eira, but her eyes were pure darkness. Somehow Eira felt more comfortable with this one. Suddenly the girl on the bed got up. "Hi! You must be the new girl? I heard about you!

Eira Tajna Candles? I heard you are special! My name is Marie Dipper, and this is my sister Lily Hallow."

Lily grunted as Marie motioned to her. When she did, her sleeves fell and Eira could see red lines on her arm. Marie followed her gaze and then smiled awkwardly and lowered her arm, letting the sleeve fall back down. She smiled brightly at Eira. These two seemed to be a few years older than Eira, so were they part of the initial experiments? And had they been separated as she and her sister had been?

Eira could feel Marie staring at her. It felt awkward, so Eira helped ease the awkward silence. "So...you have heard of me? From whom?"

"From the other facility, the inmates and Miss Cameron..." started Marie.

"And from your father..." finished Lily.

"My father?" Eira turned toward Lily. "You know my father?"

"Well, I do," Lily replied.

"How do you know him?"

"He was at the other facility with your mother. Once she recovered from her ailment, she ran it. He stayed to watch over her, I think. They seemed to have a special connection to one of the kids there. I believe her name was Magyk. I assume she was probably their daughter. I didn't know they had another one though until Marie told me..."

"How could you not know if he told you about me?"

"He spoke of a girl named Eira at the other facility he was keeping track of. Said she was special and had great potential. He was waiting for an opportunity to take some of us to collect her. I wasn't sure why he was so obsessed with an experiment at the other facility, but when Marie told me that you were his daughter, it began to make sense…"

My father was planning on coming for me? Why did he leave me in the first place, then?

Mastema chimed in. *Your father always has a plan. No one ever understands his reasoning but him and his wife. Your mother was the only one who ever understood him and got through to him.*

How do you know that, Mastema?

I know lots of things, dear one.

Eira turned toward Marie. "You said you know me from the facility? Did you mean the same one that your sister spoke of?"

Marie looked at the ground and seemed sad for a moment as she shook her head. Suddenly she looked up and was smiling again. Eira felt like this was a normal thing for this girl to always act happy even though she could tell the girl was deeply troubled. After a minute, Marie spoke, "I came from the same facility as you did."

So, they were separated like me and Magyk. Magyk…my sister… "How old are you two?"

"We are 12…" They said together.

"How long have you guys been here?"

"Roughly three years…I was dropped off here and shortly after, Marie managed to escape and ended up here."

"How did you two know you were sisters?"

"We didn't…" Marie said.

"Miss Cameron told us…" said Lily.

"How did Miss Cameron know?"

"Miss Cameron knows a lot of things…" Marie started.

"But we do not know how she knows…" Lily finished.

Eira was getting the feeling Miss Cameron knew a lot more than she was letting on and was unsure of how involved she was in all this mess. Eira couldn't tell why but she felt a strange kinship with these two. She felt like she belonged and that she was safe with these two. She hadn't felt this way since that day with Miss Cameron or her younger years with her brother. She was still unsure of how Marie knew about her since the facility kept them hidden from each other unless they fought. Had she and Marie fought before?

The sun was setting, and it was getting time for dinner. Eira knew she should meet Miss Cameron, but she still had one question left. "Do either of you know what happened to my parents?"

"Your father is fine…" answered Marie.

"And my mother and sister?"

"Your sister is alive…" Marie started.

"Your mother, we are unsure. Hopefully, she is fine as she was supposed to have more children…" Lily finished.

"How do you know that?"

"Let's just say we have a special connection with the universe. Perhaps we can show you sometime?" Marie answered.

"I would like that. But first I should go down to dinner. I promised Miss Cameron I would be there. Maybe some other time?"

"That sounds good. Perhaps we will join you. What do you think, sister?" Marie smiled at Lily.

"Fine…" Lily conceded.

They left together and went down to eat. Even though Eira didn't know it yet this would be only the beginning of her friendship with these two.

Chapter 13: Under Attack

As time went on, Eira felt happier and more at home in this place. She found comfort in the bond she had with Miss Cameron and her new friends. Miss Cameron was always there to discuss the nightmares and memories that clouded her mind and her friends all seemed very understanding. Even the inmates that didn't initially seem to like her had been friendlier to her and she was feeling at home. And even if she felt like she was alone, she knew Mastema was always there. It was weird enjoying the company of these people as she had always been alone and had quite enjoyed it before—or at least she thought she did. But now, this sense of family and community was comfortable. She had even stopped trying to find her family. She was at peace. She was home.

Eira sat at the dinner table with her friends and they were all chatting. Marie was staring intently at this rock. She seemed to carry it everywhere nowadays. She had hardly touched her food. This was unusual for her as she usually seemed to be a bottomless pit. She was sitting there with her arms stretched on the table, her chin resting on the table edge, and her eyes staring at the rock in her hands.

Eira tried to get her attention, but she didn't respond. Lily told her there was no point in trying to get her to focus somewhere else. "Why is she staring at that rock like that?" Eira inquired.

Eden shrugged. "She seems to have some weird obsession with it."

"She thinks it has magical properties or something like that," said Kas.

"Where did she get it?" asked Eira.

"She found it in the surrounding woods…" stated Lily, matter of factly. She didn't look up or make eye contact. Eira was curious as to why but decided not to ask.

"Why would she think it has magical properties if she just found it outside?" inquired Eira.

"Because she is nuts. Both of them are," said Phoenix.

Lily grunted.

"Calm down, guys. She isn't crazy. She believes it and I am sure there is a good reason for it," stated Eden.

"Just like there was a good reason she went into the woods after Miss Cameron told her not to. She could have been killed!"

"That is enough, Phoenix…" said Mastema. Everyone turned to look at her since she had been quiet until now. Everyone except Lily got up and left, leaving her plate of food on the table. Miss Cameron saw her leave and came over to make sure everything was all right. They all tried to reassure her they were fine.

"Why don't you all go back to your rooms for now. You can take your food and I will come collect it later, ok?"

They all groaned in objection but got up and left. Marie was still so out of it they almost had to drag her up to get her moving. "I just thought something would happen by now. Spring is almost over…" groaned Marie.

Eira got up to leave, too, when Miss Cameron stopped her. "I am so glad that you are making friends, Eira. It is a nice surprise to see them leaving their rooms more often. I don't know what happened just now, but I hope it was nothing serious…"

"It wasn't, Miss Cameron. I promise."

"Alright then. On your way then."

Eira turned to leave when she suddenly heard Mastema's voice. *Ask her about the rock.* Eira didn't know why Mastema thought that Miss Cameron would know about the rock, but if anyone would know about the weird rock Marie had, it would have to be Miss Cameron. She stopped halfway to the door before turning around. "Miss Cameron?"

"Yes, dear?"

"Do you know about the rock that Marie has?"

"Yes, I know of it. What is it you want to know?"

"Well, what is so special about it? She seems to be obsessed with it as of late."

"Well, spring is nearing its end. I am sure she thought something would happen by now. I keep telling her to be patient. Unfortunately, patience is not her strong suit."

"Patience for what, Miss Cameron? What does she think is going to happen?"

"She is waiting for it to hatch."

"Hatch? But it is just a rock. Rocks don't hatch."

"Well, it isn't just a rock, my dear. It only appears that way on the outside. Its magic is on the inside. Remember, you can never judge anything by its appearance as you never really know what lies beneath till you get to know it. Everything has an energy and you never know what surprises it can bring. It is a crazy and beautiful world we live in."

"So, what is she expecting to hatch from the rock?"

"A dragon."

"A dragon? I thought those were made up…"

"Oh no. They are very much real. All legends have some truth to them. If everything that will become a legend didn't exist, you and I wouldn't exist."

"What do you mean, Miss Cameron?"

"You will understand in time, dear. Now off to bed with you. It is getting late."

By now, Eira should have understood that Miss Cameron would probably not give her a direct answer. She figured it was probably something similar to the angels and demons thing they had discussed. Eira had been reading up on dragons. Humans seemed to have conflicting views of dragons. Some viewed them as monsters, usually harboring treasure or stealing away or guarding young mistresses. Others viewed them as signs of luck or prosperity or at least that is how she interpreted it. This signified the same duality of angels and demons—created the same but with opposing attributes. This probably meant that some dragons were good and others evil. She wondered if the appearance of the dragon changed its overall being. Whether it had four legs or two, wings or none, or perhaps whether it was more snake-like or more beast-like. *I wonder what kind of dragon Marie's will be.*

Eira went to the door and stopped again. "Miss Cameron?"

"Yes, dear?"

"When will the egg hatch?"

"When the time is right."

Eira didn't know what she meant but also knew she would not get any better answers, so instead, she told Miss Cameron good night and headed off to bed.

Eira awoke suddenly to a loud noise. *What was that? It sounded like an explosion.* Eira rushed to her door and opened it. She looked

91

down the hall to where the stairs to Miss Cameron's office was, but the stairs were gone and there were flames everywhere. Phoenix and Midnight were ushering everyone outside.

"Come on!" they hollered at her.

Eira didn't move. "What happened?"

"I don't know. There appears to have been some kind of explosion in Miss Cameron's office and in the back wall near the stage of the dining hall," Midnight said, grabbing her arm and pulling her toward the doors.

"Explosion? From what?"

"I told you there would be an attack, young one," said Phoenix.

They were all outside. Everyone seemed accounted for. Even Mastema was down here. The only person Eira didn't see was Miss Cameron.

"Where is Miss Cameron?"

"She is in the dining hall. She told me and Phoenix to get everyone out. She said we would need to make a run for the second facility where Project Celest is. She said she would meet us there," said Midnight.

"I thought that it had been destroyed…"

"It had been. They rebuilt when the weather got better," she explained.

"Rebuilt? Does that mean my father was found?"

She looked down. "I do not know, but Miss Cameron seems to think so. She said he would be able to help."

"Come on, we need to get going," said Phoenix.

"Right. If we head out now, we should get there by sunrise," replied Midnight.

"We cannot leave, Miss Cameron!" exclaimed Eira.

"She will be fine. She said she would meet us there," said Eden.

"Besides, we won't be any help to her. No sense in us all dying," said Kas.

Eira turned to Phoenix. "You said it doesn't matter what we did that some of us would die?"

"That is correct," said Phoenix.

"Stop this nonsense! We need to go, NOW!" said Midnight.

They all turned toward the woods, but Eira broke free of Midnight and ran back inside. "Eira!" she yelled.

She started to in after her when Phoenix grabbed her arm. She shook her head. "She will be fine. Trust me…"

Midnight sighed. She didn't doubt that Eira would be fine, but she wasn't so sure that they would be without her.

Eira ran inside the building. There was an overwhelming heat inside now that most of the building had caught fire. But fire never had bothered her. She felt akin to it as she did the shadows, and she knew it wouldn't burn her. She ran through the flames feeling their warming burn on her skin. As she crossed the entrance hall to the dining hall, there was another loud explosion above her head. The roof exploded with fire and the building began to collapse. She barely moved out of the way as a chunk of wall hit the ground. If she wasn't careful, she would be crushed.

Another explosion caused the wall between the entrance hall and dining hall to collapse. Dust and smoke erupted as the wall hit the floor. Eira swung her arm in front of her as if to clear it as she walked through. On the other side of the smoke, she saw Miss Cameron standing there. It looked like there was another collapsed wall where the entertainment stage had been. Miss Cameron said she had put it in when she took over because she had always enjoyed theater.

On the other side of the hole came what looked like an army. There were people like her. Some of the other test subjects she had heard or seen about seemed to be in their ranks. They were the older ones which explains why they were helping. They had been broken and brainwashed...like her brother.

She scanned the approaching group for him, but she could not see him, nor could she sense his presence. However, what she saw was more than just other test subjects. There appeared to be humans with them, too, she could smell them, and there were all sorts of demonic creatures with them. There were basic ones that reminded Eira of the stereotypes the humans place on their kind, like red skin or horns and fangs. Other ones were more subtle with strange colored eyes, pointed ears, fangs, or some combination of the three.

The three main ones Eira noticed were the ones she was familiar with. The large beast that looked like some prehistoric dinosaur fused with a panther with a long snake-like tail. A man with a long black cloak and what appeared to be a long-beaked bird skull on his head. He appeared to carry a staff and had a large black bird on his shoulder. And the creature with a long snake tail and human torso. He had reminded her of the depictions the humans had of a creature they called Medusa except he had 6 arms and instead of snakes for hair, his head was covered in slimy tentacles where his face was supposed to be. These three were the ones her brother always had said had a fierce loyalty to Father. If that was true, why hadn't they helped return her to him and why were they attacking the Asylum now?

Eira even noticed that some had wings. Eira thought the wings were a beautiful attribute and had always wanted them, but she had been told that if she got them, they would show up when the time was right…like Marie's egg. Why hadn't it hatched? If there was ever a time the creature inside would be needed, it would be now. Suddenly there was a roar in the sky and Eira looked up. In the sky, there was what appeared to be a lizard with wings…like the beasts she had seen in books. It was shooting fireballs from its mouth like a dragon. Was it a dragon? Was it responsible for the explosions? Why was it attacking them?

Eira wished she had time to address all these concerns with Miss Cameron, but right now it looked like they would have to fight. There was no way she could get Miss Cameron out of there without some altercation happening. Not with how close the army was now. She yelled out to get Miss Cameron's attention so she would know she was there to back her up. Miss Cameron turned her head toward Eira and made a motion to tell her to leave. "Eira, what are you doing here? Why aren't you outside with the others?"

"I couldn't leave you, Miss Cameron! You are my family!" she yells over the sound of another explosion as the building collapses more.

"Go with the others. They will need you if they are going to make it to their destination. I will be fine. I promise…"

"But…"

"No buts…I will meet you there. I promise. Now have I ever broken a promise to you, Eira?"

"No…"

The intruders had reached the building and as they swarmed in, Miss Cameron pushed Eira back through the opening in the wall that led to the entrance hall as it was covered with the pieces of the falling building. The last thing she saw was Miss Cameron standing there smiling at her the way she had been the day she first met her. Except this time, Eira could have sworn she had cat ears, a cat tail, and fangs? Was it a trick of the light? Was it an illusion made by the dust as the building fell? Mastema had told her that as they grew, they slowly changed and as their powers got more advanced, they could hide these traits. Had Miss Cameron been hiding them?

There wasn't time to worry about that. She needed to get out of the building before there wasn't a building to escape from. She needed to find the others. Miss Cameron said they would need her…but why?

As they entered the forest en route to their destination, Marie couldn't help but notice the full moon. She loved the moon, especially when it was full. Her powers were always at their strongest at night and the full moon seemed to give her a boost. She pulled out her egg and held it. Lily groaned. "Would you quit with that stupid rock?"

"IT IS NOT STUPID!"

"Would you two cut it out? This is not the time. Miss Cameron is counting on us…"

Lily folded her arms and rolled her eyes but said nothing further. They began walking again…everyone except Marie, who had noticed something different about her egg. It felt warm in her hands. She stood there staring at it. It began to move. She stared at it in wonder. "Um…guys?"

They stopped. Phoenix looked amused. Midnight was upset. "We have to go!"

"Something is happening…"

"Stop fooling around!" Midnight said angrily. She went over to Marie and grabbed her. As she did, the rock moved quicker and then cracked open. Midnight stepped back. Everyone moved in closer to see what was coming out of it…everyone except Phoenix who already knew.

Everyone gasped. Marie made an excited squeal as a little serpent crawled out onto her hand. It looked like a snake mostly, but on the upper half of its body, it had two legs with wings attached. Its head was some cross between a dragon and a snake. It was snake-like in shape and structure but had dragon-like facial features. Its scales were beautiful shades of pink and purple. It curled itself around her arm and climbed up onto her shoulder.

Everyone stared at it in amazement. Marie was beaming with joy. She turned to look at her sister. "See, I told you it wasn't just a stupid rock!"

Lily rolled her eyes and walked again. Everyone else followed, even Marie. As they walked, they heard a noise behind them. They stopped and waited. Someone was watching them. Hunting them. "Run!" yelled Midnight.

Everyone took off. They heard a scream. They turned as they saw Maddy taken by what they could only describe as a shadowy figure. Midnight had a sinking feeling she knew who it was after them. Mas screamed and ran after the shadowy figure. Midnight tackled her and held her back. "It is useless she is gone."

"YOU DON'T KNOW THAT! WE COULD SAVE HER!"

"Look at me," Midnight said, looking Mas in the eyes. "Mas, Maddy is gone. She isn't coming back…trust me. The person who is after us is relentless. He will not stop till we are all dead. We need to go…"

Phoenix nodded. "She is right…we should go…"

"I have to try…"

"You will die…" said Phoenix.

Mas looked down at the ground, tears welling up in her eyes.

Midnight looked at her sympathetically. "Let's go…"

They got up to leave, and as soon as they were a few feet away, Mas took off into the forest after the shadow figure and Maddy. Midnight turned. "Mas! NO!"

Phoenix grabbed her arm and shook her head. Midnight stomped her foot. "Damn it! I should have made sure she followed us…"

"There is nothing you can do about it now…"

Eira was running through the forest. She didn't know which direction to go like the others, but she could follow their scent and their trail. She would catch up shortly. As she got closer, she heard a scream. She ran forward, but by the time she had gotten there, no one was there. All that was left was blood…but whose? She needed to catch up with the others…

The sun was rising and they had reached the edge of the forest. They stood on the edge of the hill and looked down at where the facility should be. It was completely destroyed.

"I thought you said it had been rebuilt?" Lily asked, annoyed.

"It was…"

Lily turned to see what she was staring at. Standing in the rubble was the shadowy figure who had taken Maddy. He was standing there staring at them. All they could see was a hint of his face as his cloak covered most of him, but even his face was hidden behind a mask.

"What do we do?" asked Eden.

"We fight, of course!" exclaimed Marie.

"That would be suicide…" said Kas.

"No…you all go. I will stay. You all run. Find somewhere safe to be. Miss Cameron will find you…"

"Are you sure?" asked Phoenix.

Midnight nodded.

"If you do this…you will die…" said Phoenix.

"What? We can't leave you to die! We are staying with you!" said Marie.

"No…I couldn't save Maddy or Mas. I won't let you guys die too. I will be fine. We are old friends…him and I. Besides, even if I die, at least you guys will be safe. Now go…"

Phoenix ushered them all back into the woods, only glancing behind her, watching as Midnight approached her old friend and knowing this would be the last time they would see each other.

Eira came out of the woods. She had followed their trail out of the forest. She stared down into the clearing. There was destruction. The remnants of what was once a building and standing in the center of it was 42. And laying at his feet, motionless, was Midnight. Was she dead? Did he really kill someone he had cared so much about? When her eyes met his, she knew the answer. She knew she should stay and fight, but something else took hold, like an instinct, and she ran. When she had gotten there, she knew which direction the others had taken off, but now she wasn't sure where she was going or if she was following any particular trail. All she knew was she had to get as far away from him as possible.

She didn't know how long she had run or how deep into the forest she was. She stopped for a moment. She turned around. She didn't see or hear him anywhere. She sighed. Perhaps she had lost him. Unfortunately, she could no longer sense her friends either. She was really lost. She knew she couldn't just stay here, though. So, she turned back around. She gasped.

He was standing there, and before she could say anything, he had her by her throat and slammed her into a tree. She had been taught how to escape from attacks like this, but now the knowledge seemed to evade her. She couldn't see his face, but she could see his eyes beneath the mask and they filled her with a terror she hadn't felt before. She kicked at him, but it had no effect. She couldn't get his hand to remove from around her neck.

He smiled at her. She couldn't see it behind his mask, but he knew she could sense his humor in the situation. "Hello, little sister. Remember me?"

"Stephan..." she gasped. She could barely breathe, but he had released his grip so she could barely talk. "...why are you doing this?"

"I told you we would meet again, little sister. I told you I would come back for you, didn't I?"

She tried to nod but couldn't move her head.

"Do I ever break my promises?"

She tried to shake her head, but again it wouldn't move.

"No. Our word is all we have, after all. No point in lies. Those are for the angels. You and I...we work with the truth. I will never understand what is so fascinating about you. Why father favored you even though I was obviously the better choice. But that doesn't matter now, does it?"

Silence.

"I loved you, you know? At first, I didn't. Taking care of you was a job. But then you grew on me. I loved you. I tried to free you, but all that did was show me how pointless it really is. There is no escape for us...you or me. We will have to do what we were

100

created for. Follow Father's plan. Always…as long as we live anyway."

His expression grew dim. He removed the mask and lowered his hand. She thought he might drop it, but he didn't. She could see that his expression was serious and his hair had fallen to cover his eyes now. Yet she felt no less afraid. "Brother?" she managed to get out.

He looked up at her with an almost surprised expression. It was as if he had forgotten she was there. "I am sorry, sister."

"For…what?"

"That it has to end this way…" Tears streamed down his face. "But it is the only way to save you. I have to end your pain. I have to save you."

He put his mask back on. He brushed her hair away from her face and then leaned in close. He whispered, "I…am…sorry…"

"What…are…you…" she got out. Suddenly she felt a sharp pain in her abdomen. She could feel a warmth leaving her body and trailing down. Was she bleeding? He let go of her and she fell to the ground. She tried to say something to him, but she couldn't find the words. He stood above her, watching her. They stared at each other until everything went dark.

She opened her eyes. She was lying on a couch. Light was coming in from the window across the room. The light hurt her head. She blinked a few times, and then her vision focused. She sat up quickly. She growled a little bit as pain surged, but she didn't lay back down. A man's hand grabbed her arm. "Rest."

She looked at him. It was her father. He was crouched by the couch, looking at her. His blond hair was reflecting the sunlight. Behind him stood Levi, as always dressed in pure white like his hair. He was looking down at her with a deep concern, unlike her father. Her father's face was harder to discern, but he didn't seem concerned. Standing next to Levi was a girl in a white gown. Her hair was long and flowing, so blond it almost looked white. They looked about the same age. Could that be her sister? And if she was, where was their mother?

Eira looked at her father. "Father?"

"Yes, child?"

"What happened?"

"You were injured. Nothing to worry about, though. Levi fixed you right up. He is the best at that. You should be fine to start your training in a couple of hours."

"My training?"

"I am sorry that your return couldn't be under happier circumstances. Something has happened. Plans have changed, you understand? Now that you are back where you belong away from those humans, we need to get ready for the war that is coming."

Eira's head hurt, and she didn't remember much, but then suddenly she remembered a face...a girl? With cat ears...and a forest...then it all came rushing back. "Father? I was in a forest looking for my friends. I need to find them."

She tried to get up, but he put his hand in front of her and made her remain on the couch. "Don't worry about your friends. They are fine."

"But..."

"SILENCE!" He yelled. Then he regained his composure. "I said they were fine."

Eira could sense he meant they were alive but that he wasn't willing to expand on that. She wanted to see them, but she had a sinking feeling he wouldn't allow it. She was worried about Miss

Cameron, but she wasn't sure he would respond well to the questioning.

He tapped her leg. "You rest. I got some work to do. I will be back in a little bit. Levi will watch over you. And don't worry about Miss Cameron, either. I will take care of her when she gets here."

Was Miss Cameron going to come looking for them? For her? What did he mean by take care of her? Eira didn't think it a good idea to ask. She probably wouldn't like the answer anyway. He got up to leave. There was still one question she needed answered. "Father?"

He paused but didn't turn to look at her or say anything.

"Where am I?"

"Well, child. You are home…"

www.ingramcontent.com/pod-product-compliance
Lightning Source LLC
Chambersburg PA
CBHW030257180626
46812CB00012B/1748